Sisu

To Ted, my broker.
Happy Reading!
Joyce J. Pacheco

Sisu

[Guts, Drive and Determination]

A Woman's Journey Into A Man's World

by

Joyce J. Pacheco

www.BookstandPublishing.com

Published by
Bookstand Publishing
Houston, TX 77079
2010_3

Copyright © 2006 by Joyce J. Pacheco

All rights reserved. No part of this publication may be reproduced or transmitted in any form or by any means, electronic or mechanical, including photocopy, recording, or any information storage and retrieval system, without permission in writing from the copyright owner.

This is a work of fiction. Names, characters, places and incidents either are the product of the author's imagination or are used fictitiously. Any resemblance to actual persons, living or dead, events, or locales is entirely coincidental.

ISBN 1-58909-375-5

Printed in the United States of America

Acknowledgements

Thank you for your encouragement and suggestions:

Adolph, Shirley and Harold
Fletcher, Trudi
Jurmu, Ray
Jurmu, Steve and Kerry
Larsen, Margaret
Olson, Carolyn and Paul
Oshiro, Jay

Preface

Sisu [*See Soo*]
(Guts, Drive and Ambition)

Facing all odds, Marta a young European girl, came to New York to start a business in a "Man's World." This was unheard of in the year of 1920.

Gangsters were meeting the ferry from Ellis Island, promising naive, young girls a job with excitement, and a glamorous life, only to find themselves in the life of prostitution, better known as "White Slavery."

The "Roaring Twenties"- a time of change - fashions, music, dancing, transportation all met with a new challenge for Marta. Prohibition, Women's Suffrage, Bootlegging, and the crash all played a part in Marta's new life.

With her determination, or "sisu," would Marta weather it all to become successful in a strange new world? Had she made the right decision to leave the security of her home and family? (She missed them already.)

She would be entering a new world, where she dreamed that the streets were paved with gold. Could she find the man of her dreams - someone who would treat her as an equal? Or was this all fantasy. This was 1920. What destiny was in store for her?

v

Chapter One

The breeze picked up, Marta grabbed her hat and headed inside the ship. As she stepped inside the door, she tripped on the step. Two strong arms reached out to catch her.

"Oh, thank you," she said, as she wiggled free to catch her balance.

"My pleasure," stated Tom with a bow. "Won't you let me escort you? My name is Thomas."

"How do you do? My name is Marta. Thank you for asking, but I don't have the time now."

He tipped his hat as he left. He had noticed her as she was standing on the deck. There was something about her that fascinated him. She was soft and feminine and smelled of wild flowers - intoxicating, that was it. She was definitely intoxicating. She made him feel strong, protective and everything that a male needed to feel. When she flashed that dazzling smile, he felt empowered.

"I must try to find out more about her," thought Tom.

Thomas was returning to America from France, where he had spent a year in the Army. He was returning to his family in Upper Michigan. His father had migrated there from Finland through Canada. His mother had died of consumption, when Tom was only five. His father had married a widow with three sons and one daughter who was the same age as Tom. They wrote to each other while he was in France.

Marta hurried back to her stateroom. It was small, but comfortable. She unlaced her shoes and pushed them off with her feet, removed her hat and suit. She grabbed her robe and curled up on the bed. She searched for a letter from her aunt in

New York. She found it in her handbag. Her aunt said that she would meet her on Ellis Island. She also wrote about her thriving seamstress business and invited Marta to work for her until she could set up her dress design shop. Marta put the letter back into her handbag and closed her eyes. The gentle rocking of the ship soon lulled her to sleep.

She awakened with a start. Had she missed dinner? She glanced at her watch; it was six o'clock in the evening, just enough time for an early dinner. She quickly searched her wardrobe for a wool suit, silk blouse and gold accessories. She didn't dress formally, because it was too early. She wanted to hurry back to her room so that she could sketch more designs.

Marta looked like a dream, with her auburn hair piled up on the top of her head. Soft tendrils fell to her neck and framed her face. The white wool suit, with an emerald green blouse enhanced her coloring. She had ten more minutes to get to the dining room. She arrived a little breathless and sat at a table for six near the window. The dining room looked very inviting. All of the tables had fresh flowers, white linen tablecloths and napkins. A huge chandelier gently swayed with the movement of the ship. Outside, the sun was setting and the sea was emblazoned with the gold and orange light dancing on the water.

As Tom approached the dining room, he spotted Marta. With a bit of a tip, he persuaded the maitre de to assign him a seat at her table.

"Hi! We meet again," he said, as he sat down across the table from her.

"Hello, Tom, it's good to see you again. Don't we have a beautiful table? Look at the sunset, the colors are so vivid."

"Yes, I do like my view, I think it's fantastic," he said as he winked at Marta.

Other people joined them at the table. A young couple who were on their honeymoon, and two senior citizens sat with them. A very interesting combination, thought Tom.

They began introducing each other. They were all excited about going to New York to visit relatives. The young man said that he liked married life.

"How long have you been married?" Tom asked.

"We've been married for exactly one day," the young lady replied. Then everyone laughed.

"After you have been married for as long as we have, we'll ask again," the older couple said.

"How long have you been married?" Marta asked.

The gentleman answered, "We are celebrating our fiftieth wedding anniversary. Most of the years have been good ones, but we have had some bad times too."

The older lady said, "That's the way of married life. You have to take the good with the bad. That's how you grow. You have to learn to trust each other and to be able to communicate with each other. Never go to bed angry."

"Thank you for the good advice," said the young man. "I think that I will always remember what you have said."

The waiter took their orders. The food was served with flair, and each serving was artistically prepared. Not only that, it was delicious.

After dinner, the group went off to dance. Tom asked Marta to dance. The orchestra was playing a waltz. They looked stunning dancing together. In fact, they enjoyed each other so much that they danced all evening.

"I'm going to have to sit down and catch my breath," Marta said. So they found a table away from the crowd where they could talk. "It must have been difficult for you in France, so far away from home. Please tell me about your experiences there."

"I was in the battle of Chateau-Thierry. We stopped the German advancement in June. You know that gas was used during the war. I was one of the casualties. I was sent to a hospital in England after a short recovery period, I was sent back into the Battle of the Marne that lasted for two months, July and August. You know, we were all kids, really scared and lonesome for home. We were so happy when the hostilities ceased on November 11, 1918. I became ill again, from the gas that was used in battle. I had to be hospitalized again. Now, I'm returning home," said Tom.

"I read in the newspaper and heard over the radio about the total ruination of the historical buildings. Also, about the suffering of the children who were orphaned. Many of them were without homes and families and were left roaming the streets," said Marta.

"It was disastrous! We saw the children roaming the streets, begging for food and shelter. We helped them with our rations and any extra clothing that we had. Many of the churches took them in and helped to find families for them."

"I'd like a breath of fresh air," said Marta. "Let's go out on the deck." The wind was howling around the ship. The waves were high. The sailors on the ship asked them to go inside, because of the dangerous conditions. The boat was rocking and creaking as they found their way inside, "Thanks for the beautiful evening, Tom; I really must get some beauty sleep."

"It really is getting late. Can I escort you to your room?" asked Tom.

"No, thank you," said Marta, "I'll see you at breakfast."

Chapter Two

Tom sat in his room thinking about the evening. He was filled with thoughts of Marta. She seemed so right for him, but he wasn't ready to get serious about anyone. He had to find out where he was going from here. What, kind of work would he find? He didn't have any money to speak of. Oh, he had a little pension from the army, because he was wounded in action, but that was extra money - not enough to support a wife and family. He would eventually marry someone like Marta.

Marta thought about the fun she had with Tom as she was getting ready for bed. Yes, she really did like Tom, but definitely only as a friend, not as a lover or a future husband. She had too many things that she wanted to do. She wanted to develop her line of fashion. She didn't want to be tied down. She wanted a fresh new start in a new country. After all, her family depended upon her success. Two more days at sea and she would be landing on Ellis Island. Oh, how excited she was! She would begin her sketching in the morning - a newer softer line of clothing, and new, soft undergarments. Forget about the stiff ribs of the corset. Women wanted the freedom of movement in their clothes as well as the freedom of life. They wanted to be treated equally in the so called "Man's World."

It was raining, and the ocean swells were high. Marta had a difficult time staying on her bed, so she decided to get dressed and get some fresh air. She had trouble walking to the dining room, because the ship was swaying so much. It was difficult opening the door to the deck, because of the wind and the high waves. As wind caught the door, the rain hit her in the face and she fell against the wall. A sailor stepped forward and walked her back inside the ship. He told her to not venture outside until the storm subsides. As she wound her way toward the dining room, she noticed the long line to the infirmary. People were holding buckets and heaving into them. "Oh, I'm so glad that I don't get seasick," she said to herself. "I feel so sorry for them." The captain announced over the loudspeaker that everyone should remain indoors until the storm is over.

After a delicious breakfast, Marta wondered to the game room where she found people playing cards, checkers, ping-pong, and chess. "It's too noisy here," she thought to herself, "I'll have to find a quiet place to do my sketching." As she was drawing, she thought, "If I could only get some women together, I could have a style show. I have about ten ensembles that I could use."

Just then, Tom broke away from the poker game and approached her. She told him about her idea, and he said, "Let's talk to the purser. I'll look for him and you can see if there are some ladies who can model for you.

Tom found the purser, who thought the idea was great, and it would be a nice change for everyone. As they approached Marta, they could see that she had found four young girls that she could have to model her line.

"How soon can you get the show together?" asked the purser.

"How about tomorrow afternoon?" asked Marta.

He checked his schedule and said that it would be just fine, "Perfect at 2 p.m.?"

"Yes, can we have a serving of tea, finger sandwiches, cake or cookies, and an assortment of fruit?" asked Marta.

"I think that I can arrange that. What about music? Oh, by the way, my name is Jeff."

"It would be great if we could have live music! Do you really think that can be arranged? My name is Marta." She reached out her hand to shake Jeff's.

"I'll do some checking around, but for sure I'll be able to get a piano player and maybe some strings." Jeff said, "I'll let you know just as soon as I get things arranged."

"Thank you, very much. You have been so helpful." Jeff hurried off to arrange things.

Marta began talking with the models about the fashion show. The purser made a sign announcing it, and posted it up on the Activities Board. Everyone was passing the word around that they were going to have a new line of fashions presented to them. It was a fresher, softer look - a look of freedom - for the woman of the twenties.

Marta asked the girls to meet in her stateroom about 4 p.m. to try on the clothes and to practice for the show. She hurried to the room to begin pressing the clothes. She chose an evening gown of ice blue satin. The gown was cut on a bias so that the material would cling to the body. The sleeves were bell shaped and cut to the elbows. The neckline was cut in a V shape in the front, as well as the back. The skirt was full and came to a swirl with freedom to walk and to dance. She had the slippers to match, made of ice blue satin. She would have the model wear a long string of pearls and crocheted white gloves.

The second evening gown was made of shimmering champagne taffeta. It had a fitted bodice down to the hipline and gathered just below the waist. It had a scoop neckline in the front as well as the back of the dress. The skirt was full, and came to the ankles. The dress was sleeveless, so the model would have to wear long off-white gloves. Her jewelry would be in gold. Her shoes would be pumps in off-white color.

She quickly found two suits, three daytime dresses, four skirts and four blouses. Two of the blouses were made of silk, and two were sweaters.

The clothes were pressed and ready to go by 4 p.m. There was a knock at the door, and in walked the girls with a look of anticipation. They were ooing and awing as they tried on the garments. The clothes fit perfectly. Then they practiced walking. Everything was ready. They could hardly wait for tomorrow.

The next morning the fashion show was announced over the loud speaker. It was to be held in the grand ballroom at 2 p.m. Marta went to see how everything was shaping up. Jeff really outdid himself. There was a ramp running down the center of the room. The tables were arranged near the ramp so that everyone could get a good look at the fashions. The tables were covered with white linen with a small arrangement of pink and white carnations in the center of each table. There was the piano player, and string quartet. Marta chose the music for the occasion. The purser had arranged a large closet for the girls to use as a changing room. Tom helped to get the clothes up to the room for changing.

Now that everything was ready, Marta had to get ready. She also wore one of her designs. It was an afternoon dress - great for a tea. A yellow crepe cut on a bias that clung to her body, showing her voluptuous curves, and flaring down to the lower part of her leg – mid-calf - showing her slim ankles. She wore a string of pearls that her family had given to her as a going-away gift. Her sleeves were long, tapered, and buttoned at the wrist. She made a flower of the same material and fastened it to her waist with ribbons falling down to her hemline. She pulled her hair to one side, tendrils falling down on the opposite side of her face. She wore pearl earrings. Marta was a vision of the woman of the twenties.

Tom had made a large sign, which he placed at the entrance,
WELCOME TO MARTA'S FASHION SHOW
FEATURING HER OWN DESIGNS.

The sea was calm and passengers welcomed a diversion. The tables began to fill. The music began to play as Marta stood up to present her fashion line. "Now that the war is over, we need a fresh start - even in our fashions. We have a softer look for the twenties. Let me start with the daytime fashions. Just then, Sara entered the room with a soft print fabric of rayon, tied at the collar with a soft bow. The sleeves were gathered at the shoulder and falling gently to the elbow. The bodice was fitted and the skirt hung loosely from the waist to just above the ankles. She wore a hat with a ribbon of matching material. She wore white lace gloves, and black pumps. Sara looked radiant as she walked down the ramp and back again.

The audience clapped with delight as Effie came on the ramp. She was wearing a soft fabric of light wool. The bust line was flattened, and the belt was lowered to the hip. The hemline showed the ankles. The neckline was squared. The sleeves were 3/4 length. There was an insert of buttons just below the neckline. She wore high-buttoned shoes. The dress was plaid wool of red, white and black in color. As Effie walked down the ramp with one hand on her hip and looked very business-like, Marta said, "This is for the new business woman of the twenties." The ladies in the audience cheered and clapped.

It was Margie's turn to show off a straight skirt with an insert of pleats to the left side of the skirt. She wore a knitted sweater of white, and carried her jacket over her shoulder. The suit was made of brown gabardine. She wore a green scarf around her neck. "This is for the professional woman planning to open her own business or perhaps go to college," said Marta.

The evening dresses were a rage. The models did a super job. After the show, the passengers inquired about ordering the clothes or buying the ones that were shown. They formed a line and Marta dealt with each new client. She sold everything that was shown and had orders besides. SHE WAS A SUCCESS! Marta was on her way for a bright new future that she had dreamed about. She had enough money from the sales to buy new material.

Later that evening, a gentleman dressed in grey, came up to Marta to talk to her about her designs and possibly working for him. He was an attractive man, about six feet tall, black hair, light complexion, and clear, blue eyes. He was probably in his late twenties. She thanked him, and told him that she was interested in setting up her own shop. He asked her if he could help her financially and share in a percentage of the profits. He also talked of his idea to start a factory where he would make several dresses of the same design and market them to stores all over the United States, and later abroad. He liked her designs. He said, "My name is Ben Epstein, and look forward to working with you in the future. Here is my business card. Please call me, and maybe we can come to some kind of a business arrangement."

Marta took the card, and promised to think it over. She would call him after she had settled down in the new country.

Tom met Marta after dinner to talk about the day. She thanked him for all of his help. She saw Jeff and quickly handed him a good tip for all the work that he had done for the occasion. "It was a good diversion for the passengers," said Jeff.

After Jeff had left, she told Tom about Ben Epstein and his business proposition. Tom warned her of untrustworthy people who prey upon young women like herself. He said that men would meet the ferry from Ellis Island and promise money to young ladies who were traveling alone and sell them for prostitution. This was called, "White Slavery."

"I appreciate your concern, Tom; however, I would never meet or even call a person like this unless I checked his background. Also, my aunt would know how to go about doing this. I am more experienced than you think. I have read a lot. I'm really not that naive," she said.

"Oh, well, 'Lady of the World,' my apologies. Let's go out on the deck, the moon is out, and it's so calm after the storm," said Tom as he took her arm and walked out to the romantic evening. The stars were sparkling, the sea breeze was gentle and the moon was shining. It was hypnotic. Tom put his arms around her. She turned to face him. They looked into each other's eyes, and their lips touched. Marta pulled away. She felt strange. She wanted him to kiss her, but was afraid of the consequences. He pulled her to him again. This time with success. She placed her arms around his neck and they kissed. It was a "Kiss of Fire" - hot and sparked with passion. "Oh did you feel the sparks?" asked Marta.

"Is that what you call it? I thought it was a KISS OF FIRE," said Tom. "I think that we had better try that again. I want to see if we have the same reaction."

"Forget it," said Marta "I have to pack, and find the girls who helped me with the show today. I want to give them a gift of money to thank them."

They went back into the ship and found the girls dancing in the ballroom. Marta went up to them and thanked them. Then she gave each one of them an envelope with money in it. They thanked her, but refused to take the money. They said that it was just a fun thing to do.

Marta said goodnight to Tom. She noticed a tall gentleman in the shadows. She recognized him as Ben Epstein. She said good night to him as well, and hurried off to pack.

Chapter Three

The next day, as they were nearing Ellis Island, Marta and Tom exchanged addresses and promised to keep in touch. They were becoming fast friends, which was the way they wanted it to be. They each had many things to do before they settled down. Marta secretly smiled as she thought of the "Kiss of Fire."

Tom stayed with Marta as they entered the port on Ellis Island. She told him that her aunt and uncle were meeting her there. The Registry Room of Ellis Island was bustling with immigrants weighted down with their possessions. The main building was very impressive. It looked like a castle built in the French Renaissance period. The immigrants were inspected visually as they climbed the stairs. The people were sent to a special inquiry room if they did not answer the inspectors properly. If they were detained, they were placed in dormitories. They separated the men from the women and children.

They purchased tickets for their final destination. Women, who were traveling alone, were detained until a male relative picked them up, because of the white slavery trafficking, which was rampant in the city.

Tom and Marta went through the Registry Hall without any problems. "Look up at the balcony, Tom, I can see my Aunt Anna and Uncle John waving at us." said Marta excitedly, as Tom and Marta ran up the stairs to meet her aunt and uncle.

How delighted they were to see each other! Marta introduced Tom to her uncle and aunt, and explained how they had met on the ship and that he was a young soldier who had just come from France. They all hurried to the ferry, carrying their luggage. They were all talking at once and were extremely impressed with the Statue of Liberty.

Uncle John hailed a cab and they took it to their apartment in Manhattan. All three hurried to retrieve their luggage. Their apartment was in a row of buildings that looked exactly alike. They were called row houses.

Tom said that he would have to get a train to Upper Michigan the next day and would have to get a hotel for the night. Aunt Anna would not hear of it. She said that she had an extra room that he could stay in over night.

Uncle John hurried to unlock the door. The entrance had a mirror at one end and a coat tree next to it. Turning left at the entrance was the living room. Although it was modestly furnished, it looked warm and comfortable. The kitchen was very cheerful, with a table for serving as well as chairs to match. Most of the meals were served in the kitchen. There was a wood-cooking stove. At the top of the stove were two warming ovens. The kitchen had four windows that gave a lot of light. They were brightly colored curtains on the windows. Off to the right of the kitchen was a sewing room that also served as a guest room. Aunt Anna told Tom that he was welcome to spend the night in that room which had a daybed on one end of the room.

There was a washroom at the end of the hall. Upstairs were two bedrooms with a bathroom in between them. Marta was assigned to one of the rooms. Uncle John and Aunt Anna slept in the other one.

Aunt Anna said, "I will have dinner ready for you in one hour, perhaps you would like to freshen up and rest before dinner." Marta asked if she could help with the dinner, and Aunt Anna replied, "You can be on the 'Clean Up' committee."

Marta welcomed time to hang up some of her clothes and to freshen up a bit. She quickly took off her traveling suit and looked for something comfortable to wear. She found a pair of lounging slacks and a sweater. Then she took a quick "French Bath." She was all ready to go down in a half an hour. She was really hungry, and wanted to get down to visit with Aunt Anna and Uncle John.

She met Tom at the bottom of the stairs. He really looked handsome. He was wearing grey flannels with a red sweater. His hair was brown, hazel eyes, about 5'10" in height. When Marta met him at the bottom of the stairs, he put his arms around her and said, Marta, you look so beautiful! Then he kissed her quickly on the cheek.

"Tom, you surprised me! Let's go into the kitchen to help." They followed the delicious smells into the kitchen to find everything ready to be served.

"Pasties!" shouted Tom. "This just happens to be one of my favorite dishes. We have them a lot in Upper Michigan. In fact, they are even served in restaurants."

Aunt Anna had prepared them earlier in the day. Pasties are made of potatoes, onions, hamburger and rutabagas, wrapped with a piecrust and then baked. The vegetables are raw and the meat is not cooked until it is baked within the crust. It bakes in a 350° oven for an hour.

Aunt Anna and Uncle John had lived in Upper Michigan when they first arrived in America. So they were familiar with the area and talked readily to Tom about the different locations and people. They liked Tom right away. Tom had a very pleasing personality.

After dinner, Marta and Tom cleaned the dishes and the kitchen. As they worked together, they were talking of their plans for the future. They were only twenty years old, and had a lot of time to work before they even thought of marriage. After the kitchen was "Spick and Span," Tom asked, "Voulez-vous promenade avec moi ce soir?"

"Oui, monsieur, avec le plaisir," said Marta. "Well that's the extent of my French. Can you speak French fluently?"

"As a matter of fact, I do," said Tom, "However, some of my French should not be used in mixed company."

They both laughed. They asked Aunt Anna and Uncle John if it was safe to walk around the block at this time of the evening. Uncle John assured them that it was. "There is only one problem; will you be able to find the right house? You know, all of the houses look exactly alike. Why don't you put out the plant that is near the door? In that way for sure, you will be able to find the right house."

They were so happy to be together. They had magic. As soon as they walked about a half a block, Tom put his arms around her. She faced him and put her arms around his neck. Their lips together, and truly sparks could be felt. They really had the right chemistry. "I love you, Marta I think of you night and day. You are constantly in my thoughts."

"Tom, I know that we have magic between us, and I care a lot about you, but we are too young to become romantically involved," said Marta.

"Marta, I know that I have no right to ask you, because I don't have a job. Will you marry me?

"Tom, you have not heard one word that I have told you. We have careers to think about. I care about you, but I will not marry you, not now or in the near future. You know that my parents have entrusted me with their savings to start a fashion business. That is what I must do, before I think of my personal life. We can be friends, Tom."

They quickly walked back to Aunt Anna's house. They were waiting for them in the living room in front of the fireplace. The room looked cozy with the fire crackling. Marta asked them about their daughter.

"Helen is married to a man from Denmark. They are living in California at the present time. He's in the flower seed business. They spend half of their time in California, and the other half of their time in Denmark. They met during the time Helen was working for a Seed Company in California. They are very happy. Anker, Helen's husband is very handsome, tall and ambitious. You know Helen is also very tall. They make a very striking couple," said Aunt Anna.

Uncle John brought out their wedding pictures. "I see what you mean," said Marta. "I hope to see them some day."

"We're expecting them for Christmas, so you can meet them at that time. Tom, you're invited to come for Christmas too. Do you think that you could come?" asked Aunt Anna.

"I'll try my best," said Tom. "It depends on whether or not I can get off work Also, whether or not I have a job. Thanks, Aunt Anna, I'll try my best."

The older couple excused themselves and retired for the evening.

After they left, Tom gathered her into his arms and their lips came together like magnets. Their kisses were like fire! This was a new experience for both of them. They didn't want to talk - only to kiss each other. "I do love you too, Tom, but I need my space. I need to try to see whether or not my clothes line will succeed," said Marta. "Meanwhile, we can write to each other." They hugged each other, and Marta climbed the stairs to her bedroom.

She awakened to the aroma of coffee and fried bacon. She quickly bathed and brushed her hair to one side. She pinched her cheeks so that they looked rosy. She wore a white wool business suit, with a blue silk blouse. She looked fresh and innocent.

Tom heard her come down the stairs and met her with a light kiss on the forehead. They went into the kitchen for breakfast. Of course, Aunt Anna had a delicious breakfast of bacon, eggs, coffee, fruit and homemade cinnamon rolls. "What a feast!" said Tom, as they sat down.

"I've packed a lunch for you, too, Tom. I put a couple of pasties in the bag, some cookies that I baked yesterday, and an apple," said Aunt Anna.

"You're spoiling me, but thanks, I am very grateful for your thoughtfulness," said Tom.

They finished breakfast and there was a cab waiting for them. They all decided to go together, because Uncle John wanted to show Marta their new shop.

The train was on time. Tom bought a ticket to Chicago and then to Upper Michigan. As it rolled out of the station, Marta's eyes began to tear. She kept looking out of the window of the cab so that her aunt and uncle would not see her crying.

The shop was very close to the train station, so they gave the cab driver the address and rode about a mile away. They stopped in the front of several stores. She saw the sign in the window. MARTA'S AND ANNA'S DRESS DESIGN SHOP. "When did you do this?" asked Marta.

When we heard that you were coming, Uncle John had someone paint the sign for the shop. How do you like it?" asked Aunt Anna.

"I love it! I love it! I love it! Thank you! Thank you!" Then she kissed both of them. As they entered the little shop, there was a counter facing the door. There was a window on each side of the door to display ready-made dresses and blouses. They did not have a cash register, but they had a strong box for the money that Uncle John took care of. The shop was neat and clean. It had a warm, welcoming feeling. In an adjoining room was the workroom with two sewing machines, a large table for cutting, and a cupboard to keep the bolts of material. There was a raised platform for hemming the dresses. Aunt Anna thought of everything. Marta said, "I have some money to buy material. The family pooled their money so that we could have money enough to get started. Also, I had a style show on the ship, and many of my outfits were purchased. So I have money from that too. In all, I have two thousand dollars."

Aunt Anna and Uncle John were amazed! She was so pretty, fragile looking, but she really had a business mind.

"Let me see some of your designs," said Aunt Anna.

Marta took her tablet out of her bag and displayed her designs. "They are a softer look, with the idea of an independent woman setting out to work as equals in the male world," said Marta.

Uncle John looked at her with a surprise at the last comment. Aunt Anna studied the designs," I like them," she said. "But don't you think that you are rushing it a little?"

"I don't think so," said Marta. "The modern woman has a chance at the business world and they want to look the part."

"Well, I'll let you go ahead with your designs, but I will sew the old fashion ones. We'll cover both ends. We'll see whether or not your designs will fly," said Aunt Anna.

"A business man gave me his card after the style show on the ship. He is in the clothing business. In fact, he has a factory where he makes the clothes. Can you check him out for me,

Uncle John? He said that he has a new idea of making the dresses of one design and selling them to stores around the United States and even abroad. He is interested in some of my modern designs," said Marta.

"Yes, I can check on him. I'll have a look around and ask some of the business people whether or not he is known in these parts," said Uncle John.

Just then, the door flew open and a young blond girl ran into the room and begged for them to hide her that someone was after her. She looked like a frightened rabbit chased by a fox. Uncle John motioned for her to come into the back room and they hid her under the large cutting table.

At that moment, two unsavory characters opened the door of the shop and looked around. They pushed aside Uncle John and headed for the back room. Uncle John took them by the back of the neck and pulled them out. He said, "What is the meaning of this? Walking into a private business and pushing people around? Now you get out of here or we will call the police. There is one standing right outside of the door."

"We don't want any trouble," they said, "We have lost a girl that we bought to work for us. She got out of the cab when we stopped for a light. We thought that she ran in here."

In the first place, this is a free country; no one can buy a person for their own property. It's against the law. And in the second place, I do not see her, do you?" asked Uncle John.

"No, I don't see her, but I saw her run in here. I paid good money for her, and I have to have her," said the unsavory character.

"You know, I think we should call the police, because if you are in the "White Slavery trafficking" business, the cops would love to meet you and to hear your story," Uncle John said as he moved to open the door.

Just the then the characters ran out the door and caught the cab again. They heard them yell to the cab driver to hurry.

Meanwhile, Uncle John locked the door and they all joined the frightened little girl in the back room. She was shivering from the cold. It was November, and she had on only a thin dress. She was sobbing so hard that she could hardly speak. "I am Inga Nelson, and I am from Sweden. I came off the ship at Ellis Island and my cousin Nels was supposed to meet me. I couldn't find him anywhere, so I started walking down the street in New York City. All of a sudden, someone lifted my coat from behind and pulled it over my head. Then I was lifted into a cab. I ended up in a hotel room, where there were several other young girls who were crying. They had been kidnapped too. There were bars on the windows and the door was barred shut. There was no way to escape. We were prisoners. Today, a man came to see us. He had us stand in a row. He had us bend over, and turn around. We were wearing only underwear, because our clothes had been stripped from us. Then the man came close to each of us. He checked our teeth, felt our skin and our breasts. It was so humiliating. If we refused him, he would threaten to shoot us. He said that he wanted me for prostitution. I don't know how much he paid for me, but he threw a dress at me. Told me to put it on. Then he grabbed me and shoved me down the stairs and into a cab. I was shivering, so he threw me a blanket. When we approached the stop sign, I quickly opened the door, and ran into your store. Please help me find my cousin. Also, I want to get help to the other girls, they are in the hands of unscrupulous men. Can you help me?

"I think that the first thing that we need to do is to get you out of here," said Uncle John. "They will be back, and the next time they won't be so nice."

Chapter Four

They quickly called a cab, and found a coat to put around Inga. Then they headed for home. No one said a word in the cab, because they did not know whether or not they could trust the cab driver so they got off two blocks away. They paid him and walked into the opposite direction until the cab disappeared.

Uncle John unlocked the door. They hurried into the warm townhouse. John went around pulling down the shades and locked the doors, just to be sure that they would be safe from intrusion. Then Uncle John said that he would get in touch with a friend who lived down the street who also was a detective. He would ask his advice. While the ladies were busy feeding Inga, Uncle John left the house to look for his friend Hank, the detective.

"I'll get the bath ready for you, Inga, and Marta will look for some clothes for you to wear," said Aunt Anna, as she left the room, she made sure the doors were locked.

"Thank you so much," said Inga, "I know that God has led me to you. I will be forever grateful." She could not eat very much, because she was so weak, and hadn't eaten much for a week.

Marta hurried to her room to find the clothes for Inga. Lucky for her, they were about the same size. She found underclothes, stockings, boots, a skirt and sweater. She took everything to the bathroom for her. She even had a toothbrush and a hairbrush to give to her.

It took Inga about a half an hour to shampoo her hair, and get dressed. She felt so much better to be clean and to have something in her stomach. Most of all, she was thankful to be safe. "Shh!" whispered Aunt Anna, "Someone is coming." There was a knock at the door. Everyone was quiet, as Aunt Anna peeked out the side window where she could see who was coming and going. There was a strange man knocking at the door.

"Hi, Hank, I was just looking for you," said Uncle John.

"I had heard that you were looking for me, so here I am. What can I do for you?" asked Hank.

"Come inside, so that we can talk in private," said Uncle John as he unlocked the door. "Please have a seat, and let me introduce you to my wife Anna, my niece Marta, and a friend Inga. We are here because of Inga. After you hear her story, maybe, you can advise us as to what to do."

Inga proceeded to tell her story in every detail. After she finished, Hank asked her questions. "Do you know the name of the Hotel, or the location of it?"

"They had my head covered when they took me into the hotel, but I had a glimpse of it as I was taken away. I believe that I could show you how to get there. We must hurry to rescue the girls, before they move them to another location. I believe that I can take you to them. The best time to go would be late in the night, because the men do not stand guard at night," said Inga.

"Do you think that we should get the police involved?" asked Uncle John.

"I think that we should rescue the girls first, and then we can get the police involved to track down the men who are involved in this White Slave trafficking," said Hank.

"Do you think that we could get enough coats to give to the girls in order to get them out of the hotel? Between the two of us, we can get you six coats," said Aunt Anna.

"John, Inga and I will go and get the girls. I can pick the lock. The girls will feel safe if they see Inga and she can tell them not to make any noise. We'll enter the hotel from the rear. I think that I know the hotel that you are referring to. It's called the Black Dragon Inn," said Hank.

They each took two coats, a flashlight, and hurried off to rescue the girls. Aunt Anna and Marta stayed behind to get ready for them.

Hank had a car, so they drove it a half a block away from the hotel and down toward the back of the hotel. They walked up the stairs and moved toward the door that Inga remembered to be room #203. When they got to the door, it seemed to be all clear. Inga went to the door and whispered to the girls that she was there to help rescue them. Also, that they should be quiet, and cooperate to the fullest. Hank proceeded to pick the lock. When he opened the door, they were surprised to find only six of the girls left. They looked frightened, but as soon as they saw Inga, they were relieved. They quickly grabbed a coat they were offered, and followed Uncle John and Inga down the steps and to the car. Hank gave a quick look around to find anything that the gangsters may have left behind. They were crowded in the car, but they managed, and soon were at the door of the townhouse. Aunt Anna quickly opened the door to Uncle John's knock and call. Aunt Anna had soup ready for the girls and a hot cup of cocoa. The girls were quietly eating. They looked so grateful for the rescue.

"Now that we have rescued the girls, we must call the police they can get the gangsters who were involved in this kidnapping. They could wait in the room and capture them when they return to the girls in the morning," said Hank.

"Please tell me what happened to the other girls," asked Inga.

"When the men came back to the room informing everyone that you had escaped," said Sofia, "They decided to place us in different hotels until they could sell us to other Houses of Prostitution. Oh, by the way, my name is Sofia, and I am from Denmark. I was walking to the store and was grabbed by someone who put a bag over my head and carried me off to the hotel where you found me. I was working for the Hanson family as a nursery maid for their children. I am very sure that they are very worried about me. I have no relatives here. They hired me while they were visiting Denmark. They needed a baby sitter and I was hired for the job."

"I am Susi, from Paris, France. I came to find work in the 'Land of Opportunity.' I was staying with my Aunt and Uncle until I found work as a seamstress. I was walking down the street for a newspaper and someone grabbed from behind. They put a scarf over my head so that I could not scream. I know that my family is very concerned about me. I must let them know as soon as possible," replied Susi.

"I am Penelope, from London. I was hired for the Wright family. It was my day off and I walked to the park. As I was walking, I was abducted and taken to the hotel. I know that my family would like to know where I am. I am so thankful for the rescue.

"I am Henrietta, from England. I was hired as a maid for the Walker family. I enjoyed my job. One day, one of the servants asked to meet him near the park to introduce me to someone who could help me find a job where I could make a lot of money and that I would be able to send for my family. I told him that I liked my job, but I am interested in getting my family here. So I decided to take him up on his offer. When I met the man, I knew immediately that there was something evil about him, so I turned and tried to run away, but the servant helped the man capture me. I really believe that the servant was working for the gangsters all along. I do not believe that the family that I worked for was aware of this, because they told me that they hoped that I would stay on. They also said that they were having difficulty keeping their help."

"I am Kirsti from Finland. I came here to study at the University. I have a Fulbright Scholarship. I am studying at Columbia. One day I decided to walk to the public library when two men accosted me. They took me by the arms and forced me into an alley. They proceeded to blindfold me and tie up my arms. Then they shoved me into a car and drove me to the hotel. Thank God that you came along to save me."

"Oh, Kirsti, I am also from Finland, and so are my Aunt Anna and Uncle John," replied Marta as she ran over to Kirsti and put her arms around her.

"I must go to inform the police of what has happened, and also make a plan to break this White Slavery Ring. Please keep your doors locked and try to arrange a place for the girls to sleep. There is not much you can do about contacting your loved ones until morning. John, you stay here to protect the women. Do you have a gun? These men are dangerous and will stop at nothing," said Hank. Then he quickly opened the door and walked out into the cold night.

"Girls, I don't have beds for everyone, however, someone can sleep here on the sofa. Marta and Inga can share a bed. Also, there is a bed in the sewing room. Then the rest of you will have to make a bed on the floor. I have enough blankets for everyone so that you will be warm," said Aunt Anna.

"Oh, any place will be fine. We are safe and away from those terrible men. We can take turns in the bathroom and hurry to sleep. It won't take us long. Thanks for everything, Aunt Anna and Uncle John." I hope you don't mind us calling you Aunt and Uncle," said Inga.

The girls didn't take baths - they washed themselves quickly with soap and water. It took them about an hour before all the lights were off and the girls were fast asleep.

Uncle John was the only one who could not fall asleep. He was feeling the enormous responsibility. He heard a car drive by. He listened carefully. It soon passed, and finally he dropped off to sleep.

It was eight in the morning before anyone stirred. Aunt Anna and Uncle John were up and about in the kitchen making breakfast. Aunt Anna put her famous cinnamon rolls in the oven, and the coffee began to perk. The girls soon awakened to the delicious smells coming out of the kitchen.

Marta and Aunt Anna soon found enough clothes for the girls to wear. A car pulled up to the townhouse. Uncle John investigated, and soon found that it was the police coming up the steps with Hank. The door opened, and the girls gathered around them asking questions.

Hank spoke first, "Someone had tipped them off. No one showed up at the room in the hotel. We want to get you girls back to your families and where you were working so that they will not be worried about you, and so that you will have a place to stay. Meanwhile, the men that we are dealing with are gangsters and will stop at nothing to get you back. John and Anna are in real danger for helping. Now let's start to interrogate each of you, one at a time. Is it all right to use your kitchen?"

"That will be fine," said Uncle John.

Aunt Anna had some fresh cinnamon rolls and coffee ready to be served during the interrogation. Henrietta went first.

While Henrietta was in the kitchen telling her story, the rest of the girls were talking to Hank and to Uncle John. Some of them did not want to go back to what they were doing. They were afraid that somehow the people that they were working with were connected. Kirsti didn't have a problem. She wanted to be taken to her dorm on the campus of Columbia University.

Marta explained that she and Aunt Anna had a dress design shop where they designed and sewed the new modern dresses for the freethinking women of the twenties. The girls asked if she would have a place for them to work. Inga was very good at embroidery. Maybe she could be useful embroidering flowers or designs on blouses and on the dresses. Some of the girls already knew how to sew and how to cut out dresses from patterns. Well, this was really turning out to be like what they would need to proceed with the dress shop.

"Hold on there!" said Aunt Anna. "We don't have enough money to pay very much for help. We're just getting started. You will need a place to eat and sleep as well. As you can see, we don't have the room."

"I think that we can work it out," Uncle John replied. "We can let the girls sleep and eat with us until they get on their feet. We'll be able to produce more of our product if we have more help. Then when we sell the goods, we can pay the girls. What do you think of that?"

We'll have to check on the shop," said Hank. "We may have some problems there."

Hank stepped into the kitchen to confer with the two policemen who were interviewing the girls. They stopped and looked at Hank. "I think that we will have to call on the Walker family to find out whether or not they were aware of their servant working for the gangsters. We will make an appointment to talk to them without involving Henrietta until necessary. Maybe we can pick up the servant and he can lead us to this ring of gangsters. We might be able to make a deal with him. Now, it is very important that the girls stay here until we get this settled.

"They will be safe here."

"John would like to check his store to see if it was safe for them to go back to work," said Hank.

"You could do that, but remember that someone may be around there to follow you home to find the girls. Think it over. Someone should stay here with the girls. They are in danger," said one of the officers.

"I think that we can take care of ourselves," said Marta. "There are eight of us. If we each take something with which to use as a defense, like a frying pan, rolling pin, etc. I think we'll be all right. Hank and John will have to be careful about having someone follow them home."

The police left the house, and Hank and John left for the dress design shop. The women looked very nervous, but quietly straightened out the house. Aunt Anna went to the kitchen to prepare something for lunch. Marta went with her. Inga stayed close the front of the house so that she could detect any activity that may occur. Sofia kept an eye out the back.

As Frank and John approached the door, they could see that someone had broken the front window. They carefully went to the door. Hank said, "Don't touch anything, until I take the finger prints." John carefully unlocked the front door. Everything was topsy-turvy. Papers were scattered everywhere. Hank called the police station so that someone could come to take pictures of what had happened. "I think that they were looking for your home address."

"I can see where the girls may need our help. You take care of things here, and I will hurry home to check on them," said John.

Chapter Five

John walked around the back of the store, and left from there. After about two blocks, he hailed a cab. Then he stopped the cab two blocks from his home. He walked in the opposite direction until the cab had left in order to mislead the cab driver. As he neared the house, he noticed a lot of activity. The girls were screaming, and waving pots and pans in the air. Marta had a baseball bat that she was using on one of the men. There were three men begging not to be hit again. Aunt Anna had a gun in her hands. She had knocked the gun out of the hands of one of gangsters. She had used a kitchen chair. Uncle John quickly took the gun from Aunt Anna and told her to call the police station. The police arrived and quickly handcuffed the dangerous men. They took the men to the police station.

"You were right, Marta, when you said that you could take care of the situation. I want you to tell me all about this," said Uncle John.

"After you left, we had someone watching the front and back doors. Also, we had two girls watching from the windows upstairs. We were all very quiet. We let the men pick the lock and break in. Then we all jumped on them with pots, pans, chairs and the baseball bat," said Marta, "We really worked as a team. Those men were screaming for mercy."

"We're not out of danger yet," said Uncle John. "They won't give up so easily."

After lunch, Inga ran to tell them that someone was coming up the steps to their house. Uncle John quickly looked out the window to see two officers returning. He let them into the living room. The girls gathered around to hear the news. "We have had a lot of luck." Joe, the servant from Henrietta's place of employment was picked up. He was so scared that he told us about his contact. Joe is locked up, because he helped to kidnap several other girls that went to work for the Walker family. The men we picked up are not ready to talk. It will take a while before we are able to find the rest of the girls and to capture the White Slavery Ring. Thank God, we are beginning to solve this problem. Now we'll have to get the girls back to the homes that they were living with or to the places of employment," said Matt.

The girls were taken one by one to their respective homes. All, but Margarite, Inga, and Sofia, who did not wish to go back to where they came. Inga wanted to find her cousin, but did not have a clue as to where to look. Maybe she would place an ad in the paper; meanwhile, she needed a place to work and to sleep. Margarite, needed a job as a seamstress, and did not have a place to stay. Sofia did not want to go back to where she came, and she was looking for a place to work as a seamstress.

Marta and Aunt Anna suggested that they stay with them until they are able to find an apartment. They would be able to work for them until they can find other work. The girls were delighted. It was now late in the evening, and everyone was exhausted. It didn't take them long to fall asleep. Marta was the only one who wanted to stay up a little longer so that she could write a letter to her beloved, Tom , to tell him how much she missed him. She didn't want to tell too much about the trouble with the White Slavery Ring, because she knew that he would worry about her. She did tell him about the shop and about the three girls who would be working for them.

After breakfast, Uncle John, Aunt Anna, Marta, Inga, Sofia, and Margarite were off to the store. They were anxious to clean up the mess, and repair the broken window. After cleaning up, Uncle John went to buy a new window. The girls sat around the table in the back room to make plans. Marta did the organizing. She said that one person would be in charge of the cutting, another for designing, Inga would be doing the crocheting, and two people would be doing the sewing. Aunt Anna would be in charge of collecting the money and do the counter work. All of the girls agreed to this. They agreed upon a salary. They were anxious to get started. Marta showed a design that they would be working on. She said that anyone who would like to make a suggestion about working conditions, or patterns or anything about the business would be welcome. Inga told them that she was also good at embroidery.

Everyone was busy with their various jobs and before long, it was lunch lime. Aunt Anna had packed a good lunch of fruit, sandwiches, and cookies. She also had coffee in a thermos.

The girls cleared everything from the table and they gathered around for the luncheon. It tasted so good after a morning of work. Uncle John had just replaced the window. He cautioned the girls to be very careful, if they needed to go out for anything, to be sure to travel in pairs.

There was a bell attached to the door so that they could hear if anyone was entering the store. The bell tinkled. Uncle John went to answer the door. It was a gentleman who asked for Marta.

Uncle John called Marta to come to the front of the store. Marta was amazed to see Ben Epstein standing there with his hand out to shake. "How nice to see you, Mr. Epstein. Let me introduce my Uncle John to you. Uncle John, this is Ben Epstein, the gentleman that I spoke to you about We met on the ship. He's also in the clothing business. How can I help you, and how did you find me?"

"I was driving down the street, and I saw the sign. I wanted to know for sure that it was you. I would also like to offer you a proposition," said Ben.

"Well, I would like for my Aunt Anna and Uncle John to hear your proposition too," said Marta.

"I am interested in buying some of your designs. I will pay you for each design, and give you a percentage of each garment that you design that I sell. Here, I have a contract for you to read. Take your time, and perhaps you would like an attorney to look over it with you," said Ben.

"Well, that sounds fair," said Marta. "I will call you when I am ready for you to pick up the contract."

"I will give you three days. I need to get started, because I have already contacted stores to carry my line. You can keep your shop here too, Marta. The designs that you sell to me must not be duplicated at your store. OK?" asked Ben.

"I will give you my answer in three days. You may come by the store at noon on Friday," responded Marta.

Ben handed over the contract; and left the store. He looked very business-like and very handsome. Uncle John and Aunt Marta were very impressed.

Marta said goodbye to Ben and went to the back room to talk with Uncle John. "Do you know an attorney that we can hire to go over the contract?"

"Yes, I do," said Uncle John. "In fact, I will call him today. We can meet him tomorrow morning before we open the store." So Uncle John called his attorney and made the appointment for the following day.

"This will give us an opportunity to go over the contract, before our meeting. Also, we can check on the man's character," said Uncle John.

Marta and the girls quickly continued their work. The garments were looking great. Sofia was embroidering delicate flowers on a white panel that would go down the front of a dress. The other two girls were busy cutting and sewing new dresses. Marta was busy with her sketching. She was also developing soft undergarments as well as lounging pajamas. They weren't bothered by anyone. You could just hear the hum of the sewing machines and the humming of Marta. She loved to hum while she worked.

They decided to walk home this evening. The night air was crisp, and snow was gently falling. They only lived about a mile from work. As they walked, they talked about all of the things that they did that day. You could see their breath as they were talking in the cool night air. A horse and sleigh came down the street overflowing with young people who were singing Christmas Carols. "I can't believe that it is almost time for Christmas," said Aunt Anna. "I have a lot to do."

As they approached their home, they noticed a light in their townhouse. "Did you leave a light on Uncle John?' asked Marta.

"No, I didn't; in fact I checked to see that everything was off before I left, this morning. Let me go ahead and check to see who may have entered our home, and then I will whistle for you," said Uncle John.

The girls huddled together. Shivering in the cold night air, and worried about the intruder. Uncle John went ahead to see who had entered their home.

Uncle John whistled. The girls went to the townhouse. Uncle John explained what had happened, "I found this note from Hank, stating that he had found the back door open. He went into the house to see whether everything was in place. He found it as it is now. Then he locked the door from the inside and left a light on."

"It's possible that whoever came in, heard Hank coming, and left," said Uncle John. "I'm afraid that it's not over. I will add a dead bolt to the front and back doors this evening. You can't pick that lock," said Uncle John.

"I'll run upstairs to see if everything is in its place," said Marta.

"I'll come with you," said Inga.

Marta and Inga ran up to check on things. Everything seemed all right. So they went down the stairs to help with the supper. Aunt Anna was in control, she was a superb cook. She quickly put a meat loaf in the oven along with some scalloped potatoes. Then she proceeded to peel some apples so that she could make an apple cobbler then she placed this in the oven too. Marta was in charge of the salad. She peeled some carrots, shredded them and added some raisins. Then she opened a can of pineapple, drained out the juice, and mixed it in with the shredded carrots and raisins. She then mixed some cream, and honey together to pour into the salad mixture.

The other girls were on the cleaning crew. They cleaned up after the cooks, washed the dishes and set the table. After an hour, they all sat at the table to partake of the delicious food. Before they ate, they thanked God for His bountiful blessings.

After dinner, Uncle John, Marta, and Aunt Anna sat in the living room to go over the contract. Marta agreed with most of the contract, except for the part that Ben would put his name on the styles. She felt that she should have the label on each garment that she designs. She would have to discuss the rest of the contract with the lawyer in the morning. She kissed her aunt and uncle and went upstairs to bed.

The next morning, there was a pounding on the door that awakened everyone. Uncle John quickly put on his pants and shirt and headed down the steps. He looked out the window to see the two police officers who had been to the house previously. As he opened the door, the officers quickly entered. "We need to speak to the girl, Inga. It concerns the other girls who were at the same Black Dragon Hotel when she was there."

Uncle John went upstairs to get Inga. She had already heard the commotion, and quickly dressed and rushed downstairs. The other girls did the same. They all met in the kitchen to talk.

"We think that we found the other girls," said Matt, one of the officers. "The girls and the men were caught at the Canadian boarder. They called us to come and pick them up. We need someone to come with us to identify them. Inga, can you do this for us?"

"Of course, I can. I'm so happy to hear that the girls are finally safe," said Inga. "When would you like to leave? It will take me about a half an hour to finish my bath and get dressed."

"That will give me enough time to make some breakfast for everyone," said Aunt Anna. She quickly mixed up a batch of pancakes, heated some maple syrup, and a pot of coffee.

The officers welcomed a good breakfast as they had been working since five o'clock in the morning. It now was seven a.m. The girls were bathing and getting dressed for work, while Uncle John sat and talked to the two police officers. He told about the door being open and the fact that Hank had found it that way. They told them to be careful, because they had only caught three of the men and they weren't talking. Now that the Canadian Mounties had two more men and the girls, they may be able to get to the bottom of this.

"Will Inga be in danger?" asked Aunt Anna.

"She is in a precarious position, because she can identify these men; however, we will be with her and plan to give her the protection that she will need. The two men that she has to identify will be put into jail as soon as we return. We plan to have a paddy wagon carry them back. Inga and the girls will be riding with us. I believe there are about five more girls. We'll each have to drive a car," said one of the officers.

"I'll ride with Matt, if that's okay with everyone," said Inga.

Matt gave a nod of approval. He was a tall, broad shouldered man with auburn hair. He looked like an Irishman. He was about twenty-three years old. His eyes were blue, a ruddy complexion, and a fantastic smile. Inga thought that he was handsome, and she was right. Inga and the officers left for the police station where they would pick up another car and the paddy wagon for the two gangsters. It was an ominous day. The skies were grey and threatening.

Soon Matt and Inga were on there way to the border where the girls were waiting. The girls were huddled together. They all brightened up when they saw Inga. At first, they were frightened when they saw Matt, the Police Officer. Inga assured them that they were here to help them. Matt took care of the paper work and they all went to the cars. Inga and Matt took three of the girls, and the other officer took the other girls in his car.

Inga told the girls that the girls who were left in the hotel room had been saved. Also, that they had been taken to their respective homes. The officers decided to take the girls to the station to question them about their abduction and to help them to locate their families. Inga decided to stay with the girls until all were settled, and safe.

The two gangsters decided to help the police round up the other men in the White Slavery Ring, in order to get off at a lesser charge. They also asked for protection until all were captured. They were promised protection for information.

After everything was taken care of, Matt asked Inga if she would like to go out for dinner. Inga said that she was famished, but needed to freshen up a bit. Mart drove Inga home. Uncle John, Aunt Anna and the girls were just arriving from work. Matt told them all about the day while Inga ran upstairs to freshen up and change her clothes.

Aunt Anna invited them to have dinner with them, but Matt declined. He wanted to take Inga out for dinner so that he could thank her for helping and to get to know her better. He really liked Inga; in fact, he was attracted to her.

Matt had changed his clothes at the Police Station, so he was wearing a pinstriped suit and Inga was wearing a suit that she had sewn since she was working for the shop. It was a royal blue suit. She was wearing a white turtleneck sweater. She had crocheted a matching white hat and gloves. She looked stunning! Her blond hair had been cut to a shoulder length. Her hair was natural curly and the curls fell right down to her shoulders. Her pale blue eyes flashed with anticipation. As she came down the stairs, Matt was waiting for her. He said, "Wow! You look great! It didn't take long to get ready."

Uncle John gave a whistle. "Is that the suit that you were working on for the last two days?" asked Uncle John.

"Right on," said Inga. "Thanks to a lot of help I got from the girls."

"Yes," said Aunt Marta, "We help each other. We have a great team here."

"I won't keep her out too late," said Matt.

"She's in good company," said Uncle John, "We won't worry about her, but don't keep her out late."

"That's a promise," said Matt.

Matt was a perfect gentleman. He opened the door for Inga. Then he went to the driver's seat. After he started the car, he reached over to hold Inga's hand. She smiled and took his hand. They drove quietly along in his car. (He left the police car at the station.)

"There is a nice quiet restaurant not far from here," said Matt, "it's a Ma and Pop restaurant and the food is delicious. It features Irish stew."

"I thought that you might be Irish," said Inga. "I'm Swedish, you know."

"How did you learn to speak English so well?" asked Matt.

"We had to study English in High School and my mother was fluent in English. She always spoke to us in English so that we would become bilingual," said Inga.

"Here we are," said Matt, as he drove into the parking lot in front of the restaurant.

He walked around to open the door for Inga. Then he took her arm as they walked up the steps. He opened the door for her as they entered. "Hi Matt!" shouted the man who was cooking.

"Hi Pop!" said Matt. "I want you to meet a friend of mine. Inga this is my father. Where is Ma?"

"Happy to meet you, Inga," said Matt's father. "Your mother stepped in the back pantry for some supplies."

"You didn't tell me that we were going to your family's restaurant, Matt," said Inga.

"Hi Matt!" said a redheaded woman coming into the dining room, as she ran to give him a big hug. "Who is this lovely girl?"

"This is Inga, Ma, she's a friend of mine," said Matt.

"I'm happy to meet you," said Inga. "The pleasure is all mine," said Matt's mother.

"Inga and I have been working on a police assignment together," said Matt. "I think that we have almost taken care of a White Slavery Ring. Inga has helped to bust up this ring. We are celebrating tonight."

"Have a seat at this table near the fireplace, and look over the menu, I'm sure that you are famished," said Matt's Mom.

They sat near the fire. They both chose the Irish stew, and a hot cup of coffee. They also had a nice piece of chocolate cake for dessert. They talked about food that they each liked. Inga talked about apple strudel, and other Swedish foods. Matt asked whether she could cook. She said that she knew how to cook only Swedish food, but she was willing to learn how to cook other kinds of food. She explained that they were taking turns cooking at Uncle John and Aunt Anna's house.

Matt's parents kept to the background, and did not interfere. They liked Inga, but they had many questions to ask Matt after he takes her home.

"Goodnight Mom and Pop, I'll be home in a half an hour." Matt said, after dinner.

As Matt drove Inga home, he put his arm around the back of the seat and asked her to sit a little closer. It was cold so she had a good excuse to sit closer. She said, "You know, I'm a little cold over here, so I'll scoot up and sit closer."

"Good," said Matt, as he put his arm around Inga.

When they reached Uncle John's and Aunt Anna's, there was a light left on the porch. They quickly went up to the door, and Uncle John opened it. "Just in time," he said. "I was just getting ready to go to bed." Then he winked at Matt.

Matt said goodbye at the door, and said that he would see her tomorrow at work

Inga smiled at him and said that she would be looking forward to it.

Chapter Six

The next day Marta and Uncle John met with the attorney about the contract with Ben Epstein. He read over the contract. Then he made some suggestions. He suggested they ask for a higher percentage and use Marta's name on the labels. Ben Epstein was willing to give her 10% on each garment, and he suggested that she get 25%. Then he suggested a meeting with Ben Epstein and making the changes then have them all sign the necessary papers. They asked the lawyer if he had heard of his garment factories. The lawyer said that he had heard of them. He would do more checking for her. They shook hands and said that they would arrange a meeting with Ben.

At noon, Ben arrived to collect the contract. Marta and Uncle John met him. They suggested a meeting with their lawyer who was just a block away. Ben agreed. Uncle John went to the back room to call Judd White, the attorney. He agreed to see them immediately. They all went to the attorney's office.

Ben read over the changes in the contract He did not agree to the 25%, but agreed to 20%. They all signed the contract and shook hands on it Ben invited them to visit his garment factory. So they got into his car and went to see it. They were very impressed. It was a large room with twenty-five girls working sewing machines, and several girls cutting out material. "How many employees do you have?" asked Marta.

"I have fifty all together. Look over here, Marta; if you want to work here for part of the time, I have an office for you." He took them into a small room with a lot of windows; it had a desk and a drawing board for her to draw her designs. "How do you like it?" he asked.

"I love it," said Marta." I will spend half of my time here, because there is so much room for me to sketch my designs, and also to make sure the dresses come out the way I had planned."

"That's great," said Ben. "I was hoping for that, but I didn't want to take you away from your Aunt and Uncle's store."

"I'll be working there too," said Marta. "I'm looking forward to working with you, Ben."

"When can I look forward to your coming?" asked Ben.

"How about Monday?" asked Marta.

"Fine," said Ben. "I was hoping that you would have dinner with me tonight so that we can talk over our plans and when I can expect the designs from you. Also, I really would like to get to know you better."

"I'll be glad to have dinner with you, if you would invite my aunt and uncle along. I would like them to get to know you better too," said Marta.

"That will be just fine. I will have my chauffeur pick you up at seven. Please dress formally, as I plan to take you to the Waldorf Hotel. I know that you like to dance, Marta. So wear your dancing shoes," said Ben.

"We'll be ready," said Uncle John.

Ben drove them back to their store, and said that he was looking forward to the evening.

Matt and Inga just arrived back from lunch as Uncle John and Marta returned.

"I'm really excited about my work with Ben!" said Marta. "I can hardly wait for this evening. It sounds like so much fun."

"Let's all go to the back room and hear all about the garment factory, and about this fabulous evening," said Aunt Anna. They all went to the back room and sat at the table to hear about all the exciting things that involved Ben and Marta.

"I'll help you with your make-up and hair," said Margarite. "What are you going to wear?"

"I think that I'll wear the cream and gold silk that I have been working on all week," said Marta. I just have to hem it, Sofia will you help me with the hem?"

"I'd love to," said Sofia. "Put it on and I will pin up the hem for you. Do you want it floor length, or to your ankles?"

"I'd like to show my ankles," said Marta. "Let's scallop the hemline. Then maybe Inga can embroider the scallops. What do you think of that idea, Inga?"

"I really think that the embroidery would be too heavy for the material, but I will be happy to hem the dress for you," said Inga.

They soon had the dress ready. The dress was cut low to reveal just the top of her bust line. It was cut full, with cap sleeves. There was a train of silk gathered at the neckline in the back and hung down to the ankles. She would wear long gloves to complete her outfit.

༻✦༺

It was five o'clock and time to end the day at the store. They caught a cab to their townhouse, and got ready for the evening.

"I wish you were all coming with us," said Marta.

"Oh, I forgot to tell you that we have all been invited to visit Matt's parents' restaurant this evening. You, Aunt Anna and Uncle John will have to take a rain check, but Margarite and Sofia can come with us," said Inga.

"That's great," said Marta, as she hurried upstairs for a bath and to get ready for the great evening.

Margarite followed to help with her hair and make-up. "I'll get everything ready for you," said Margarite. Being from Paris, she knew all about the new hairstyles. In fact, she could even cut hair without a problem. She wanted to cut Marta's hair into one of the latest fashions.

Margarite was a petite size, with pretty, black hair, olive skin, and flashing brown eyes. She was very happy with the shop and her new friends; however, as soon as she saved enough money she wanted to get her own apartment. She would ask Sofia to join her, so that it would not be so crowded for Uncle John and Aunt Anna.

As soon as Marta came out of the bathroom, Margarite was ready for her. She had her scissors ready. "What are you planning to do with the scissors?" Marta asked.

"How would you like a new haircut?" asked Margarite.

"I'm not so sure," said Marta. "Maybe you could cut a little, but not too extreme."

"Okay, but don't watch me cut." said Margarite.

"Oh, no, I have to watch. Remember, I don't want you to cut it too short. Just to my shoulders and cut it so that it frames my face," said Marta.

So Margarite proceeded to give her a modern haircut. Her hair was naturally curly so it just fell in curls all over her head.

"I bought some make-up at the store this morning," said Margarite. "Let me see what I can do to get you ready for your big evening." She then applied the make-up. It looked very natural and tastefully done.

Marta then dressed for the occasion. She put on the undergarments that she had designed, then put on her stockings and gold sandals. She wore gold earrings, necklace, and bracelet. Then she found a long green velvet cape that she had designed. All was ready; Aunt Anna and Uncle John were waiting for her at the bottom of the stairs. She looked like a vision, as she came down the stairs with her new haircut, and clothes.

There was a knock on the door and in walked Matt to pick up the girls for a night at his parent's restaurant. Aunt Anna asked him to sit down and wait for the girls, because they were so busy helping Marta, that they were not quite ready.

Just then, Inga called down that they needed another ten minutes. Matt said that was fine and to take their lime.

Another knock at the door. Uncle John answered the door. It was the chauffeur to take them to the Waldorf. They said good-by to Matt, and yelled up to the girls. They said that they were ready too. So they left at the same time.

Uncle John was wearing a black suit, shirt, tie and vest. He put on a top coat to keep out the cold December weather. Aunt Anna wore a floor-length dress of light blue wool.

She had long sleeves, high neck and a bustle. She still wore the traditional styles.

When they reached the hotel, the chauffeur helped them out of the limousine, then they were ushered into the hotel. Ben met them at the entrance and walked them to the dining room. He was wearing a tuxedo. He took Marta's arm and walked with her to the maitre de. Then they were ushered to a beautiful table arranged with fresh orchids, near the dance floor. There was an orchestra playing softly. Ben helped Marta with her cape, and Uncle John helped Aunt Anna with her long coat.

When they were seated, Ben looked at Marta and said, "Say, I really like your hair. You are really going modern, to stay in tune with your designs. Are you wearing some of your fashions?"

"Of course, Ben, I need to promote my designs," said Marta.

After everyone was seated, Ben said, "I hope you don't mind my suggestion, but the pheasant under glass is superb."

They all agreed. Ben ordered apple cider to celebrate the occasion of a partnership with Marta. He would have ordered champagne but liquor was not allowed during Prohibition. They all toasted to good luck and health. 'Why don't you order for us this evening?" Uncle John suggested. You are familiar with the menu."

They started with hors d' oeuvres. The waiter brought a lazy Susan laden with seafood. "Yummy!" said Marta. "You must have known that we all enjoy seafood."

"I assumed as much," said Ben. "After all, you come from Finland, where your main source of food is from the sea."

After the delicious meal, Ben ordered Cherries Jubilee, because he remembered how much Marta enjoyed them on the ship.

The band began playing a waltz Ben asked Marta for the dance. She accepted with delight. They looked striking together. They danced for about a half an hour. Then Marta said. "Let's sit down and talk for a while."

They joined Uncle John and Aunt Anna at the table. Marta wanted to talk about the business. She said," Ben, I am introducing lingerie in our store. It is a softer look. I'll bring in some samples on Monday."

"Yes, I would like to take a look at your designs, Marta," said Ben. "After I see your designs, I will start advertising and sending out salesmen to the stores."

"I am really looking forward to this business venture, Ben," said Marta.

"We may have to hire more help," said Ben. "Do you know of anyone who would like to work for us?"

"I just may have someone for you," said Marta, thinking of the girls that were rescued from the White Slavery Ring. "I'll check on this for you and give you an answer on Monday." Ben asked Marta for another dance. "Of course," she said.

Ben complimented her on her dancing. As he held her close, he whispered, "How lovely you look, Marta. You make me feel so good to be holding you in my arms."

Marta had mixed feelings. She liked being with Ben, but she did not have the same spark that she had when she danced with Tom. Maybe this would change after she got to know him better, she thought.

"It's been a lovely evening," said Uncle John, "We have to get home to the girls. Also, we have to work tomorrow."

"The evening went by so fast that I hadn't realized how late it was," said Ben.

"Let me help you with your cape, Marta, then we will all go to the door where my chauffeur is waiting."

"I'll say good-bye here," said Ben. "It's been a wonderful evening. I'll see you on Monday morning at 9 a.m. sharp, Marta."

"Yes, I'll be there with all of my designs. Thanks for the beautiful evening. Everything was just perfect," said Marta.

Uncle John and Aunt Anna shook Ben's hand and thanked him too.

Everyone was quiet in the car on the way home. They were thinking of the fantastic evening. They were tired too. When they reached home, the chauffeur opened the doors and walked them to the door. They thanked him and said good night

Uncle John and Aunt Anna hurried in to check on the girls. They were all in the living room asking all kinds of questions. Marta told them all about the meeting with Ben, and the beautiful hotel. Also, that the food was the best that they had tasted.

Marta asked the girls about their evening. Margarite said, "I think that we have a romance on our hands. Inga and Mart seem to be fascinated with each other."

Inga said, "It's true. I think that I am in love with Matt. It happened so fast, but he has asked me to marry him."

"You have just met," Aunt Anna said, "I think you should give it a little time. Get to know each other first. Take your time, you're still young."

Inga went to Aunt Anna and put her arms around her, "Thank you for your concern, Aunt Anna. I will give it a little more time, but I know that I love Matt, and he loves me. I have dated before, and have not felt the same. When he kisses me I feel like there is magic."

It's time for us to go to sleep now, we have a big day tomorrow, "said Uncle John.

Chapter Seven

The next day, Aunt Anna was talking about the plans for Christmas. "We'll have to get some dresses ready for the holidays," said Aunt Anna. "Do you have some in mind, Marta?"

"Yes, I do. I have some formal wear and street wear in mind. In fact, I'm going shorter too, about mid-calf "said Marta.

"I have been crocheting some hats and gloves that we can put up for sale. Also, I have embroidered some blouses that the girls sewed last week," said Inga.

"If I can get Hank to take me up to the Adirondacks to pick up some pine cones and pine boughs, I can develop some center pieces," said Uncle John. "I'll also look for some holly to brighten up the centerpieces."

"That sounds like a great idea," said Aunt Anna. "Margarite and Sofia will be busy with the cutting of patterns and sewing. It looks like we will be very busy. I'm planning on putting an ad in the newspaper too."

Uncle John got a hold of Hank and they made plans to go to the mountains on Sunday. Aunt Anna packed a large lunch and off they went Hank, Sofia, Uncle John and Aunt Anna fit snugly in his car. Sofia sat in the front with Hank. Uncle John and Aunt Anna snuggled together to keep warm and just to be close. Marta had a lot of work to do so she stayed at home. Inga had a date with Matt, and they had a date for Margarite. They went for a ride in the country to look at the countryside.

Marta could hardly wait for Monday. She just loved her place of work at the garment factory. She sat with her sketchpad and developed styles for the holidays. She also continued with her lingerie. Before she knew it, she heard a car stopping outside.

It was Hank and the group that he took with him to the mountains. They were weighed down with evergreens, pinecones, red berries and a number of other things to help Uncle John with the centerpieces. On the top of the car was a pine tree that they could use for a Christmas tree. They were all laughing and talking as they came up the walk Marta quickly opened the door to let them in. "Everything smells so good! It smells like Christmas," said Marta as they placed everything in the hallway.

Aunt Anna invited Hank to have dinner with them. They had a very light dinner, because everyone was anxious to decorate the Christmas tree. Uncle John made a stand for the tree. Aunt Anna went to the closet upstairs to get the box of Christmas ornaments and a skirt to put under the tree. She also brought a bag of fresh cranberries that she had purchased from the store on Saturday to string on the tree. Hank and Inga went into the kitchen to pop the corn to string on the tree. Soon the tree was decorated in strings of popcorn and strings of fresh cranberries. Also, Aunt Anna had candles to place on the tree. She had a long candlesnuffer to snuff out the candles when they got too low. They each took turns to handle the snuffer. Then Marta went to the kitchen to make some taffy. They all buttered their fingers to pull taffy after it cooled enough to handle. Aunt Anna had a pot of coffee on the stove, and brought out the Christmas cookies.

Just then, there was some noise outside, and in walked Margarite, her date, Sofia and Matt. "Look what you have done!" said Margarite. "You should have waited for us. Oh, well we're ready for the dessert. I would like to introduce you to my friend, Josh. He's on the police force with Matt"

Everyone shook his hand and welcomed him to the gathering. Margarite went outside to the back porch, which was enclosed. "I have a surprise for you. I made some fudge the way my mom made it in France."

The fudge was delicious. They had a wonderful time talking about the way they spent their Christmas in their homeland. "I have an idea," said Marta. "Why don't we have a potluck dinner? Everyone bring a favorite dish of food that would represent their country."

Everyone agreed. "Maybe we can invite the other girls to come over too," said Sofia.

Matt said that he would see if he could get in touch with the other girls. "I'll ask my mother if we can have the dinner at our restaurant. We'll have more room there," he said.

They all left by ten o'clock feeling very festive. Monday was a busy day for all of them.

༺༻

After dropping off Aunt Anna and the girls at the store, Uncle John and Marta went down to the garment factory. Uncle John did not feel that Marta was safe to take a cab by herself. It was still a man's world, and crime was rampant in New York City, even though the 19th amendment had passed and women's suffrage was strong. When they arrived at the garment factory, Ben met them at the cab. He said, "I will have my chauffeur pick you up and drive you back each day. There is no need to pay for a cab; in fact, he can drive you back to the store, John."

"That would be great," said Uncle John as he said goodbye to Marta.

Ben and Marta walked into the garment factory. Marta had her suitcase full of the samples that she had prepared to show Ben. Also, she had her designs with her. She was walking on air! She was excited, she loved her new place of work.

"You and I have a lot of planning to do together," said Ben. "Why don't we meet in my office?"

They walked in the room right across the hall from Martha's office. It was a beautiful room with a soft rug on the floor. He had a fireplace on one wall with bookshelves on each side of it He had a long conference table in the middle of the room, and his desk was at the end of the room. "Let's sit at the table so that we can spread out your designs," said Ben.

Marta walked to the table and took out her first design. It was an evening dress for the holidays. It was fitted to the waist, gathered skirt, off the shoulders, plunging neckline, and long sleeves. "This would look good in red or green velvet," said Marta.

Ben looked at the design. "This should be a big seller. Let me see the rest."

She proceeded to show all of her designs for the evening. Then she took out the daytime dresses, the skirts were at mid-calf. He said, "A bit daring, but we want to appeal to all ages. Let's call in the rest of the help so that we can get going .on this line."

"Before you do that," said Marta, "I would like to show you my line of lingerie. This will be good for gifts for the holidays."

"Yes, please do," said Ben.

Marta showed her lounging pajama, which was a full pant leg gathered at the waist with elastic waistband. She had a loose top cut with sleeves to the elbow. The next thing she brought out was a brazier. Before this time, the women were just wrapping their breasts with strips of material. She made the bra into a cup that made the breasts stand up. "Wow!" said Ben. "You are really ahead of your time Marta, but I like your ideas." Then she showed him the panties, which were short, made of silk with lace on the legs.

"Marta, you are unbelievable. I love your aggressiveness in style. Now are we ready to call in the pattern cutter?' Ben asked.

"I'm ready, if you are," said Marta.

They had their meeting with the pattern cutter, and the supervisor. The workers were very receptive to the new ideas. They took the designs and went to work. They said that they hope to have her check the dresses in the morning. Then they would decide how many they would make of each design.

It was almost lunchtime. Ben asked her to have lunch with him. "That would be fine," said Marta. "Then I will have to hurry to the store to help my aunt and uncle."

Ben chose a restaurant near the garment factory. It was a cozy place with a warm fire crackling in the fireplace. Marta ordered a turkey sandwich, and a cup of soup. Ben did the same.

"Are you going to have difficulty getting the material for the dresses?" asked Marta.

"I have a good stock of supplies," said Ben. "I would like to have you help me buy the next supply. You have a good eye for the right material for the right design. I'll show you what I have when we get back to the shop," said Ben.

"I do enjoy buying my own material," said Marta," I'm anxious to see what you have. Where do you buy your material?"

"I take a train south, to the Carolinas where they have mills for us to purchase these materials," said Ben.

"I won't be able to go with you alone," said Marta, "I think my Aunt Anna would like to go the mills, or maybe my Uncle John would like to go. I will have to ask one of them. We'll discuss this tonight."

"I didn't expect you to accompany me alone, Marta," said Ben, "I have too much respect for you; however, you do not need to be afraid of me."

"I know that, Ben. I feel very comfortable with you. In fact, I look forward to working with you. We have so much in common. We both like nice things. And, we're both interested in clothes," Marta said with a warm smile.

"Would you like to go with me to see the ballet, The Nutcracker, on Friday night? I just happen to have two tickets," said Ben.

"I would love to go with you. Do you think that you could get two more tickets? We could ask Inga and Matt to go with us," said Marta.

"I was hoping to have a date with you alone," said Ben, "but I guess that is asking too much."

"Maybe later, Ben, right now, my aunt and uncle would not let me do that. After I get to know you better, OK?" asked Marta

"I suppose so," answered Ben despondently. Then he gave Marta a big smile and squeezed her hand. "What about the man that you were with on the ship, Marta?"

"We're just friends," said Marta. "He lives in Upper Michigan. He said that he might be here for Christmas."

They finished their lunch and hurried back to the factory. Ben showed Marta the material that he thought would be good for the dresses. Marta agreed, but she said that she needed softer material for the undergarments. "Do you think that we could go to the Carolinas in January?" asked Marta.

"That's a good idea. Well have to work with what we have at this time," said Ben.

"I'll have to go now," said Marta. "I really hate to leave. I am looking forward to working in my office. I love the skylight and all the windows for working at the drawing board."

"I don't like you leaving either," said Ben, "it's so nice having you here. I know that the girls will have questions to ask about the styles, etc."

"I'll get things in order at the store, and starting tomorrow, I'll work longer," said Marta.

"All right," said Ben, "I will be looking forward to that."

Ben's chauffeur drove Marta to the store. Uncle John was working on the Christmas wreathes and centerpieces. Inga was busy crocheting. The back room was humming with the sound of the sewing machines. It looked like Santa's workshop. Aunt Anna came over to give Marta a hug, and asked how things were going at the garment factory?

"We really got a lot of things accomplished," said Marta, "but I'll have to spend more time there to get the girls started with my new styles."

"Are you sure that is the only reason that you want to stay?" teased Aunt Anna.

"Well, I do like the room that he has for me to work. There is so much light with the skylight and all the windows. I have a drawing board too, which is helpful," said Marta. You don't need me here as much, because you already know how I want the styles to look. By the way, how many dresses do you have ready for the big sale on Saturday?"

"We have ten dresses ready. Inga has five tarns with scarves and matching gloves. Come on, we'll show you," said Aunt Anna. They walked into the back room and looked at the dresses that were ready for the sale. They were all street clothes.

They needed to make some ball gowns. Also, they needed to work on the lingerie.

"You are really doing a great job!" declared Marta. "I can see what I need to work on. I need to work on the new bras. That should be a big seller."

◈

Ben could not keep from thinking of Marta. He had that strange feeling every time he was near her. He wanted to be with her. "I think I'll drop by the store this afternoon," he thought, "I forgot to ask her to the Christmas ball on Saturday night" Anything to get to be near her again. "I don't know what has gotten into me. I've never felt like this before. Could this be love?"

Ben got out of the car at the store. Uncle John was busy working with the holiday wreathes and Christmas centerpieces.

"Oh hello," said Uncle John. "How can I help you, Ben?"

"Let me see what you are doing," said Ben. "That's a beautiful piece of work. It looks like the whole family is talented."

"Hi Ben," said Marta coming into the room, "I thought I heard your voice. It's nice to see you."

"I forgot to invite you to a Christmas ball on Saturday night, Marta. There will be a lot of prominent citizens at the ball. You can show off one of your designs. I could introduce you to some very important people," said Ben.

"That sounds like a good business opportunity," said Marta. "Of course I'll go."

"Come into the back room and see what we are doing," said Marta.

Ben went to the back room, and was impressed with all the dresses that the girls had completed in such a little time. "You have a real Santa's workshop here," he said.

After seeing what the girls had done, Ben left regretfully. He just had a sick feeling when he had to leave Marta. "I'll see you in the morning, Marta, and don't forget I'll need you all day."

"That's what I'm planning on," said Marta. "I'm looking forward to it."

Ben drove back to the factory and supervised the work that was being done. He also looked at the orders that would have to be met before Christmas. Then he drove home. He had a beautiful home on Long Island. It was tastefully decorated, but did not have the woman's touch. He wanted to show it to Marta and see what she would think of it. He started the fire in the fireplace and sat down in his easy chair. He asked the cook to bring a cup of tea and biscuits. He sat staring into the fire and thinking of Marta. He thought of how wonderful it was to work closely with her. He thought of her fragrance. She smelled of wild flowers. Her beautiful smile, sparkling eyes, creamy complexion, soft auburn curls, and the way she walked. When she laughed her voice sounded like bells. "Oh my! I really have it bad. What am I going to do? I have to take it easy or I will scare her off!" Ben thought.

Marta was thinking of Ben. She really liked being with him. They had so much in common. This was going to be so much fun. But there was more to it than that. She liked the way he chuckled when he laughed. She liked the way he dressed. His voice was very low and soothing. She liked the way he handled his business. In fact, she really liked him. Then she thought of Tom. She thought of his kisses of fire. She did not really have anything in common with him. All he could think of was getting married. She was looking forward to a career. She did not want marriage at this time.

That evening, she received a letter from Tom. He had a job with a railroad company. He was planning to be with her for Christmas. Marta put the letter back into the envelope. She was not as excited about having him visit. She knew that he wanted to get married. "I'll have to write to him and tell him that I will be too busy to entertain him at this time. That my line of clothes is taking all my time to get ready for the sale before and after Christmas."

Aunt Anna came up to Marta, "What's wrong, Marta?" she asked.

"Tom is planning on coming here for Christmas," said Marta. "I don't think that I want him to come."

"Let him come, Marta," said Aunt Anna. "You will be able to make a comparison between Ben and Tom. Tell him that you only have two days to visit, because business is so demanding."

"All right, but I know that he wants me to marry him, and I am not ready to do that," said Marta.

After dinner, Marta wrote to Tom. She explained that she did not have much time, but she would be happy to see him. In the morning, Uncle John mailed her letter.

Ben's chauffeur was waiting for Marta as she opened the door. She was very anxious to get to work where she could be in her new environment, and get her fashions out. Ben met her at the door. "Hi, Marta! Did you have a good evening?" asked Ben.

"Actually, I had a little problem that I had to take care of when I got home," said Marta.

"What was that?" asked Ben. He wanted to hold her in her arms and take care of everything.

"I received a letter from Tom. He is planning of visiting me during Christmas. I answered his letter, and told him that I would be very busy and would have one day to visit with him. I really wish that he would not come, but Aunt Anna said that it was not polite to ask him not to come when she had invited him when he was here," said Marta pouting.

Ben put his arm around her shoulders, and said, "I wish he wouldn't come too, because I had planned to invite you to meet my parents at that time."

"The letter has been sent. I have a lot of feelings for you, but I do not want to rush into anything. I think about you a lot, and love being with you, in business as well as socially," said Marta.

"I can't get you out of my mind, Marta. I think of you constantly. I like your enthusiasm for the business. I like your aggressive way in styles. I don't want to frighten you, Marta, but I think I'm falling in love."

They walked into his office. Closed the door, and he held her in his arms. Then he kissed her tenderly. He said, "Forgive me Marta, but I just couldn't help myself" It was a warm, tender kiss, not a hot passionate one.

Marta pulled away. She looked at Ben. "Oh, Ben, that was the nicest thing that you could do. I wanted you to do that" The kiss was tender; she liked the tingling that it left on her lips.

"Do you mind if I kiss you again?" Ben asked as he moved toward Marta. She walked toward him and they embraced. He kissed her with more passion this time. Marta pulled away.

"Ben, this won't work. You know that we are in business together. We'll have to not mix business with pleasure." Marta said.

"Let's sit down on the couch," said Ben, "I just want to hold you in my arms. I haven't felt this way about anyone else before."

They sat down on the couch together. Marta put her head on his shoulder. They just sat close together. "There is so much that I want to tell you," said Ben. "I want to take you to my home and show you around. I have a large home on Long Island. It really needs a woman's touch. It needs your warmth, Marta. I have a cook and butler who takes care of the place for me. Will you come home with me after work? I will have the cook fix up something special for us. I can call her. We won't be alone. What do you say?"

"Ben, I feel so comfortable with you. Do you think that we could leave early so that we can watch the sunset together?" asked Marta. "Of course we'll have to stop by at the store to tell my aunt and uncle."

He squeezed her hand, and kissed her again. "Marta, you have made me a very happy man. Don't forget, you never need to be afraid of me. I would never take you sexually unless we were married and that you would want me. I have that much respect for you."

"Thank you, Ben, I trust you with all of my life," said Marta.

"As much as I hate to let you go, Marta, it's time to go to work." He gave a big sigh as he opened the door. He watched Marta as she walked across the hall to her office. She went right to her drafting table and pad of paper to begin designing.

She left her door open for the workers to come and go as the need presented itself. They had a lot of questions about the material and the cuts of the dresses. She had a group of girls working on the lingerie.

Ben went across the hall to invite Marta into his office for lunch. He had ordered Chinese food for lunch. He had his table ready and the two of them enjoyed having lunch together. Ben closed the door, and went behind Marta. He kissed her on the neck. Marta laughed, because it tickled her neck so much. She turned around and hugged him. Then she said, "Ben, I think that we have to be careful here at the factory. We don't want the workers to start talking, and imagining all sorts of things."

"Of course you're right. It's so difficult for me to keep from holding you and kissing you. I'll have to restrain myself. It won't be easy, because of the way I feel towards you," said Ben

After lunch, they went right back to work. Marta looked outside and it looked like it was going to storm. The wind was beginning to blow. She continued to work, until about three o'clock. Then she looked out again. She crossed the hall to talk to Ben. "I think that we should quit work early, because it looks like it may snow."

"Oh, I'll have the workers close early too," said Ben. "I'll go and tell them to finish up by 3:30 p.m. Then we'll leave."

Ben locked up the factory and the chauffeur drove them to Uncle John and Aunt Anna's store. It was just a little way down the street. The chauffeur opened the door and they quickly ran into the store. "Aunt Anna, Ben has invited me to his home to dinner. He lives on Long Island."

"I have a butler and a cook at home, so we won't be alone," said Ben.

"It's beginning to storm outside, don't you think that it would be better to wait until another time?" said Uncle John.

"I've already called the cook, and she is preparing a special dinner for us," replied Ben. "The clouds look ominous, we had better get started."

"You know, Ben, I think that Uncle John and Aunt Anna are right. We had better plan this on another day. I'm really sorry; I was looking forward to seeing your home."

"I'd better get going then," said Ben. "Marta, would you please walk me to the car. I need to talk to you about something."

"I have a better idea," said Marta, "Why don't you drive me to Aunt Anna's and Uncle Ben's home, because I really don't need to stay at the store. Is that o.k. with you Aunt Anna?"

Aunt Anna agreed to let her go on home. She knew that they wanted to be together for a while longer.

As they sat in the car, the wind was blowing drifts across the street. The young couple sat very close together and held hands. "Ben, maybe you should consider getting a hotel in town tonight. I'm worried about you driving through this storm."

"We'll drive for a little while, and if it seems too dangerous, we'll stay in town," said Ben. "Come closer, Marta. I'm going to miss you so much."

It was difficult for the driver to see in the blizzard. They soon arrived at the house. "We'll have to hurry, or we'll be caught in this blizzard," said James.

Ben took Marta up to the house, and entered with her. Then he took her into his arms and kissed her. "Marta, I won't be driving home tonight. It's too dangerous, and I don't want to become snowbound. James and I can stay at the factory. I have a shower there and there are two couches in my office where we can sleep. We have so much work to get out before the holidays, and I couldn't stand to be away from you for very long."

"Why don't you send James for the girls and my aunt and uncle," said Marta. "You stay here and help me get ready for dinner. Okay?"

"Are you inviting us for dinner?" asked Ben.

"Yes, I am. James is invited too," said Marta.

Ben went out and explained to James what the plans were. James sighed a breath of relief because he was afraid that Ben would try to make it to Long Island tonight. Ben ran back into the house as James went to the store to pick up the group over there.

Marta was getting everything ready for dinner. She decided to make some beef stew, because it seemed like the thing to do on a night like this.

"Would you like me to start a fire in the fireplace?" asked Ben.

"Please, do!" shouted Marta from the kitchen. She looked so domestic in her frilly apron. Her cheeks were rosy from the chill outside and the excitement of cooking for Ben. While the stew was cooking, she decided to bake some biscuits.

After the fire was lit and crackling, Ben went into the kitchen to help Marta. He came up to her and hugged her from behind. She turned around, and he kissed the end of her nose. "There," he said. "I just kissed the flour from the end of your nose. You are so beautiful. Your cheeks are all pink and your green eyes are dancing. I didn't know that you know how to cook too."

"Yes, my mother taught me how to cook," said Marta. "She's still in Finland, you know."

I am saving money so that I can send for my parents and three brothers. They pooled their money to help me get started in the garment business. I can't let them down. I'm anxious for them to meet you, Ben."

"I'm anxious to meet them too. You will have enough money soon, Marta. I just know that our business will grow fast. In fact, when we will be able to stock our merchandise in several stores there will be a lot of money to be made. I'll bet that by next summer, you'll have enough money to bring them to the United States," said Ben.

"Oh, I hope so," said Marta. "I miss them so much. When I think of them, I feel like crying. What about your parents, Ben? Do they live near here? I would like to meet them sometime."

"You'll meet them at the ball on Saturday night, if the weather clears up. They are planning to come to the ball. They live in Connecticut. My dad was in the garment business too. Now he's retired," said Ben. "My mother helped him get started. They worked together to get the business going. Then when my mother had me and then my sister, she stayed at home to raise us. You'll love my family Marta, as I know that they will love you."

"That will be exciting to meet them. Will your sister be coming with them?" asked Marta.

"My sister is busy with her family. She lives in California with her husband and children. Now with the holidays she won't be able to join us. You know that we are Jewish, don't you, Marta?" asked Ben. "I noticed that you have a Christmas tree to celebrate the birthday of Jesus Christ."

"Yes, we are Christians, Ben. I believe in Jesus. I pray to Him every day to guide me and to thank Him for all that He has provided for me. My family goes to the Lutheran church. I haven't found one to attend here in New York, but I am looking for one."

"I have been raised Jewish. We don't believe that Jesus is the Son of God or the Messiah. We are still waiting for Him," said Ben.

"How sad for you, Ben. He's real, and He lives. He loves you too, Ben. Maybe I can show you how much He means to me, and why we celebrate his birth at Christmas time," said Marta.

Just then, the group came in from the store. "It smells very good in here," said Uncle John. "Thanks for sending James after us, Ben. It was difficult seeing the road, but he managed."

Soon the table was set, and Aunt Anna took over in the kitchen. They all gathered around the table, and Uncle John said, "Let us thank God for His blessings, for the food and for the guests that we have with us this evening." They all bowed their heads and held hands, and said the prayer in Jesus name.

After dinner, they talked about their business and about the sale that they would have on Saturday. James got up and said that they really should be leaving, because the storm did not seem to be letting up. "Oh, I forgot to call the cook and butler to let them know that we wouldn't be home because of the storm. I'll call them from the office," said Ben. He shook everyone's hand and Marta walked him to the door. He reached over to her and kissed her on the cheek Marta said, "I'll see you at the factory in the morning, o.k.?"

"I'll be waiting for you," said Ben.

Aunt Anna called Marta into the kitchen to talk to her. "Marta, I need to talk to you, because your mother and father are not here to advise you. I'm glad that you did not go with Ben to his home. I know that it looked perfectly harmless, but your reputation is at stake. Men are different from women, Marta. They are easily excited and often have a difficult time with their control. You have to be in control. Do not go to his house unless you have someone else with you. Now, I know that you care a lot for Ben, because you have the same interests. He is very handsome, and cares a lot for you. Don't get into compromising positions. It's up to the woman to set the limits. A man will try to go as far as he can in order to make you want to make love with him. You know what may happen if you go all the way? You could get pregnant. That would be an embarrassment for the family. You must be strong enough and bright enough to know when to stop when the man feels amorous. Don't let any man touch you sexually until you are married. If you let him, he will lose respect for you. Most men want a virgin for a wife. You have to find out more about him, Marta. Do you have the same religious background? You know that could present a problem if you get married."

"Aunt Anna, I really respect you. Thank you for being so honest with me. My mother did speak to me about the same things. In fact, she said not to let a man touch you sexually until you are married, even if he does it on the church steps after the wedding ceremony. She also told me that there is very little to prevent pregnancies."

"What about Tom, Marta? He'll be coming to visit you during the Christmas holidays. How do you feel about him?" asked Aunt Anna.

"I like Tom a lot, but he is getting too serious. He wants me to marry him and move to Upper Michigan. I'm not ready for that. I want to proceed with my career. I have more of a passionate feeling when I kiss Tom; however, I know that it is not enough to form a marriage. I realize that passion soon fades in a marriage that holds no other interests," said Marta.

"Have you and Ben ever spoken of marriage asked Aunt Anna.

"No, we have been so busy talking about business that we have not even considered that He did tell me that he wanted me to meet his parents. They will be at the Christmas ball on Saturday night. He is Jewish, Aunt Anna. Do you think that would be a problem if we should decide to get married?" asked Marta.

"It's a big problem, Marta. You know that he does not believe that Jesus Christ is our Savior. The Jewish religion is looking for the Messiah. They believe that He will come sometime in the future. We believe that Christ is the Messiah. If you have children, would you raise them as Jewish or as Christians? You need to discuss this with Ben, if he should get serious about getting married," said Aunt Anna. "We can talk about this another time, right now, we all are very tired. Good night Marta we love you and want the best for you." Marta hugged her aunt and went upstairs to bed.

The wind howled all night. By morning, there were large drifts of snow on the streets. Uncle John decided to walk to the store so that he could get things ready for the sale on Saturday. They all put on their boots and bundled up in order to combat the snow. The wind had died down and the snowplows were working to clear the streets. Marta soon noticed James coming up the street in Ben's car. He drove up and offered them a ride. By now, the streets were plowed and driving was clear. James let Uncle John and the ladies off at the store, and proceeded down the street with Marta to the clothing factory. Marta had a lot to think about. She definitely would set the limits, and not show Ben too much affection. When she arrived, Ben greeted them at the door. He looked a little sleepy, but had showered and shaved. He smelled really good of Old English aftershave lotion.

As she walked into the door, Ben asked her to come into his office. The fire was crackling in the fireplace. "How well did you too sleep last night?" asked Marta.

"Not too well," said Ben. "James snores for one thing, and I couldn't sleep, because I was thinking of you. Marta took off her coat and fur-lined boots. She sat down at the table. Ben poured her a cup of delicious coffee.

"What's on the agenda, today?" asked Marta.

"Well, the first thing that I want to do is to give you a hug and a kiss. I've missed you so much. I really enjoyed having dinner at your aunts and uncle's home last night. We had a terrible time making it back to the factory. The drifts were pretty high, but James is a terrific driver. So we made it. What did you do after we left?"

"My aunt and I had a long talk," said Marta. "She wants us to take it easy."

"I know that I have been coming on too fast, Marta, but I'm really taken with you. We have so much in common with the garment business and all. We will take it day by day. I know that we do have some enormous differences. For example, the fact that I am Jewish and that you are a Christian. We can talk about that at a later lime, right now, we have to get the fashions ready to show. Friday night we will be going to the ballet Every time that I take you out, you will be showing your fashions. Soon the ladies will be asking you for your designer. We'll tell them that you are the designer. On Saturday night, I shall be so happy to escort you to the ball. Oh, by the way, what are you wearing?" asked Ben.

"Saturday night, I plan to wear a light blue velvet gown. It is fitted at the top, long sleeves and gathered at the waist. There is an insert of white lace in the front of the bodice, where Inga has embroidered snowflakes. The neckline is high, but scalloped. The sleeves are long with scallops at the hand, and three pearl buttons to keep the wrists tight. I'll wear a choker of pearls, and earrings," said Marta.

"What will you wear for a wrap?' asked Ben.

"I'm not sure yet - maybe a cape. I have a fur-lined cape that I brought from Finland," said Marta. "It's getting a little worn; I'll have to check it out."

They made their plans for the day and set to work Marta was definitely aloof. She didn't want to show much affection toward Ben, especially at work. The clothing line was coming along just beautifully. His workers asked her questions about any problems that would come up. At noon, Marta left to help at her uncle's store. She was just in time for lunch with the girls. After lunch, they set to work and to get ready for the sale on Saturday. Marta pitched right in and sewed buttons on and did anything else to help. The front room of the store was filled with Uncle John's wreaths and centerpieces for the holidays. He even put candles in some of the centerpieces. Marta praised him for his artistic talent.

On Friday, when she went to the garment factory, she went to her desk and found a large package from Ben. She opened it, and to her amazement, she found a floor-length white mink coat. She ran to find Ben. He was in his office, looking quite pleased. "Ben! You shouldn't have!" shouted Marta. "Why not?" questioned Ben. "Aren't you my favorite business partner? Come on Marta, try it on. I want you to be the Bell of the Ball."

Marta hurried to Ben as he held up the coat, it fit perfectly. The collar stood up, the back was full, and the sleeves were full too with a cuff at the wrist. It felt so soft and comfortable. Marta went to the mirror that Ben had in his office over the couch "It's beautiful! Ben, I don't know what to say. It's an expensive gift. Our business is just getting started."

"I know, Marta, just call it a 'welcome to the business' gift. It obligates you to nothing. I wanted to do this for you, because I know that you needed something to wear on Saturday night when we attend the ball. I want you to make a statement. You will be wearing your own fashions. Also, I want to introduce my parents," said Ben.

"Thank you, Ben. You are wonderful! I do want you to be proud of me," said Marta.

She went to him, threw her arms around him, and kissed him on the cheek. He closed the door, pulled her into his arms, and kissed her tenderly.

"Darling, Marta, I love you so much. I want to be with you always. Then he kissed her on the neck.

"Oh, Ben, I feel so safe with you. I do thank you for my beautiful coat and for helping me to get started in the garment business. You know how much it means to me and to my family in Finland." Then Marta put her arms around Ben's neck and whispered, "Ben, I love you, too."

Then Ben kissed her with more passion. The radio began playing, "Why Do I Love You?" They pulled away and gazed into each other's eyes, as they listened to the music. They gently swayed to the music.

Then Ben said, "Guess what? We have six stores ready to pick up your fashions. Let's go to see the finished product."

They walked to where the garments were hanging. Marta looked at the tag on the inside of the dress, and noticed the tag read, "Marta's Design."

"Well, how do you like it?" asked Ben. "Don't they look grand!"

Marta called the supervisor over and thanked her for the fine job that she and the girls have done. Also, that they completed the work so fast.

Ben said that they would have a Christmas bonus, for the fine job that they had accomplished. The supervisor said that she would tell the girls. When she walked back to the girls Ben and Marta heard a loud cheer. Ben was good to his employees.

Just then, six men came into the factory to pick up the merchandise. They first examined the fashions. They looked at the seams, and the material. They were very pleased with what they saw. Then Ben called them into the office for their invoice and they each gave him a check "You have a fine line of fashions," said one of the men.

Then Ben said, "I want you to meet the designer. This is Marta. She designed all of the fashions. She also has a line of lingerie that we will present to you in January."

"How do you do?" said Marta. "I'm glad that you like my fashions. Please keep us informed as to how your patrons like them."

"It's a pleasure to meet you too, Marta. We do like your fashions and we are anxious to get these into the stores before the holidays. We'll keep you informed. I know for sure that my store will need another shipment before long." He shook Marta's hand, then he shook Ben's; we'll be seeing you soon. Then they rolled out the garments to their awaiting vans.

After the factory was emptied of all the completed frocks, Ben breathed a sigh of relief. I'm so glad that we were able to meet the deadline. Do you have any designs for capes or coats, Marta?" ask Ben. "I'm anxious to keep the girls busy until the holidays begin."

"As a matter of fact, I do. Come into my office and I will show you the sketches that I have made," said Marta. She went to the drawing board and Ben followed. "Here is the first sketch of a cape that I have made. It is made of velvet and lined with satin. The next page is a jacket made of wool and lined with lamb's wool. The next page you will see a coat. It would be pretty in red or green velvet. It has a hood, a yoke in the upper back and gathered to make the coat swing when the person walks in it. This coat would come to the mid-calf."

"I really like the styles. You really have a flare for this work, Marta. Let's call in the supervisor and explain to her what we are planning on doing," said Ben.

They called her in and explained the work that needed to be done. Then Marta said that she would have to go back to her uncle's store to help for the big sale on Saturday. "What time will you be picking us up for the ballet?"

"We'll pick you up by 7 p.m.," said Ben. "I'll be counting the minutes until I will be with you again."

"See you soon," said Marta as she hugged Ben and kissed him on the cheek.

James drove her to the store. She got out and thanked him. The store was bustling with putting everything in order for the sale in the morning. The girls were putting the finishing touches on the garments, and Uncle John put red ribbons on the wreathes and centerpieces.

They were all ready for the next day by five o'clock. Uncle John ordered a cab and they all walked slowly out. They were so tired that they could hardly lift one foot in front of the other. When they reached home, they all collapsed on the couch. Marta carried her large package into the house. "What do you have in that package?" demanded Aunt Anna.

"You'll never believe what I have," said Marta as she opened the box and revealed her precious gift. "This is a 'welcome to the business' gift from Ben. He wants me to make a statement when I go to the ballet and to the ball. He says that I will be advertising my fashions, so it is important for me to wear it. What do you think of it?"

"It's really beautiful. I'm sure that it was very expensive. Are you sure that you want to accept this gift from Ben?" asked Aunt Anna "Oh, yes, I do. He said that it does not obligate me to him. It's just a nice gesture on his part. He wants me to have it," said Marta.

"In that case, I guess it is okay, Ben is a real nice person. I'm sure he means well," said Aunt Marta. "What time is he picking you up? Inga and Matt are going with you, right?"

"Inga, did you tell Matt about the ballet?" asked Marta.

"Yes, he's going to pick me up and take me to the theatre. Ben already gave him the tickets for the ballet," said Inga.

"You better hurry then, it's already six o'clock," said Aunt Anna.

Marta led the way upstairs. She carried the coat with her. She decided to wear the green velvet dress. It was floor length, fitted, long sleeves, v-neck with a slit up to the knee. They took turns in the bathroom. Marta called up Margarite to come up and please help her with her hair and make up. Margarite fixed her hair in ringlets all over her head. Her make-up was flawless. She wore a string of pearls around her neck and a button pearl earring on her ears. She wore green satin slippers.

Margarite helped Inga get ready too. Inga had her hair cut really short; in fact, it was cut about two inches above her shoulders. She had the prettiest blond hair. Margarite used a brush and teased her hair a little to make it stand out. Then she fixed her make-up. She wore a dress to her mid-calf Bloused top and a pleated skirt, along with long pearls down to her waist. She wore a cape with fur lining. She also wore long gloves. Her shoes were black leather. She looked very modern in one of Marta's fashions.

There was a knock at the door and Uncle John answered it. In walked Ben with a white orchid corsage for Marta to wear. Aunt Anna called up to Marta She came down the steps looking sensational. She was carrying the coat. She saw Ben at the bottom of the stairs and she said, "Oh! What a beautiful corsage. Thank you Ben. You think of everything. I'll put it on after we get to the theatre." Ben helped her with her coat.

They said good night to everyone and hurried to the car. "Marta, you take my breath away. You look absolutely stunning. I'm so happy to be your escort." Then when they got seated in the car, he pulled her to him and kissed her tenderly.

Marta kissed him back, and said, "I'm proud to be with you, Ben. You look so great in your tuxedo; I haven't been to the theatre since I arrived in America. I'm so excited!"

"It's exciting just being with you, my darling! Now when we get to the theatre there will be many people that I know. I'll introduce you as my dress designer and business partner. We'll do that during intermission. "Ben looked out of the window at the snow. The night was clear and bright. "Look, the first star of the evening. Let's wish on it."

"What did you wish for, Marta?" asked Ben.

"If we tell it won't come true," said Marta.

"Okay we'll keep it a secret. Someday I'll tell you, when it comes true," said Ben.

James the chauffeur said, "We're here." He got out and helped Marta and Ben get out of the car. Marta was carrying her corsage. When they got into the theatre, Ben helped her with her coat and pinned the corsage to her dress. It looked lovely against the green velvet of her dress.

They were escorted by the usher to their seats in the theatre. When they reached them, they noticed that Matt and Inga had already arrived. They said hello in a whisper. Just as they began the music, the lights lowered and Ben took Marta's hand.

The ballet was beautiful. Marta enjoyed the music and being with Ben. At the intermission, they went to the mezzanine where they were serving hot coffee and tea, and cold drinks like apple juice or orange juice. This was the year of prohibition and no alcoholic beverages could be served. Ben introduced Marta to several young couples as his designer, and business partner. Several of the women asked if she was wearing one of her designs, which she replied in the affirmative. Ben introduced Inga and Matt too. Ben said that Inga was wearing one of Marta's designs as well.

Marta and Inga excused themselves to go to the Powder Room. When they got into the room, several women that they had previously been introduced to surrounded them. They wanted to get a better look at the dresses and to find out how they could get in touch with her to design some clothes for them. Marta very tactfully told them that they would have to make an appointment with Ben. She told them that she would be glad to meet with them at Ben's garment factory.

One of the ladies stepped forward and said, "I heard that Ben was manufacturing dozens of the same design in his factory to be sold in the department stores. We don't want to be seen in the same dress at the parties that we will be attending."

"Oh, I do designs for the individual too. If you tell me that you want the fashion that I design for you to be one of kind, I'll be happy to do that for you. You can select the material also. I'll speak to Ben about this. I'm sure that he'll be happy to accommodate you," said Marta.

"I think that it's time to join the men," said Inga. "It's been nice talking to you."

"Yes, I'm looking forward to helping you," said Marta. "By the way, Inga works with me too. She does the embroidery work for the designs that I work on."

They all hurried out to the place where the men were waiting. The ladies followed and went to their escorts. Marta went to Ben, took his arm, and went back into the theatre. Marta said to Ben, "Wouldn't it be fun to take some children to see this ballet Do you have some friends with children?"

"I was just thinking, wouldn't it be nice to take our children to the ballet," said Ben

"Ben you're such a tease," said Marta.

"Ben, the ladies approached me in the Powder Room about making some fashions for them. They mentioned that they would want a fashion designed just for them, and not a fashion that are to be duplicated like the ones we are selling to the department stores. They said that they would not want to see someone else with the dress that I design for them. I told them that I would talk to you about this. I said they would have to talk to you concerning this so that they can make an appointment.

"I have thought about that too, Marta. It depends on whom we are catering to, for example, the ladies that you met tonight, and the ones that you will meet at the party will have to be treated in a different way. We will talk more about this tomorrow. Of course, they will have to pay more for an individual design." Ben winked at her and the music began to play as the lights dimmed.

The evening went by quickly, as they were driving home, Ben said, "You don't have to work at the factory tomorrow, you know. I close the factory on Saturdays and Sundays. But of course if you want to come, I'll be glad to open up for you."

"Tomorrow will be our big sale at Uncle John's and Aunt Anna's store.

Maybe you would like to come and help out?" asked Marta.

"I have to visit the stores that are handling our merchandise and to check on how the sales are doing. Maybe I will get more orders. I will stop over after that," said Ben.

"Good! I'll be looking for you," said Marta.

"How am going to be able to get along without seeing you in the morning? I will miss you very much," said Ben as he hugged Marta a little more. "I'll pick you up at 7 p.m. tomorrow night for the ball. I'm so anxious for you to meet my parents. I know that you will love them as well as they will love you."

James stopped the car and went around to let them out. As he was walking around, Ben kissed Marta. Then he walked her to the door. Marta said, "Thanks for a beautiful evening. I'll be looking for you tomorrow."

"See you tomorrow, my darling. It's been wonderful sharing the ballet with you tonight. Sleep tight," whispered Ben.

Everyone was excited about the big sale at the store. At 9 a.m. the door opened and several people came in to shop. By noon, all of Uncle John's centerpieces and wreaths were gone. The crocheted hats, gloves and scarves that Inga made were all sold, except one set. Women were trying on the dresses in the back room. It was a very busy morning.

By noon, the place was still busy, but most of the merchandise had been sold. Uncle John decided to close the doors for lunch and to check to see whether they had enough merchandise to sell to merit keeping the store open for the afternoon. Aunt Anna checked the money drawer and they had $500 that they had collected for the merchandise. They all were happy about the busy morning. They figured out how much they needed to pay out for expenses. After paying the expenses and paid the girls, they had $100 profit. They were pretty happy with that. The girls were happy too. Margarite and Sofia were planning to look for an apartment so that they would not be crowding Aunt Anna and Uncle John.

After lunch, Ben stopped by to see how the sale went. He looked around and saw that the store looked pretty empty. "It looks like you have had a bit of luck today," said Ben.

"Yes we have," said Uncle John. "It looks like we'll have to hire a couple more girls to help with the sewing. I think that we'll have to buy another sewing machine too."

"I think that I can let you have one of mine," said Ben. "I have an extra one at the factory."

"Well, let's close up shop for the day. I think we all need a break," said Uncle John.

The girls quickly picked up and straightened out the store. Then they climbed into Ben's car and hurried home. Ben said goodbye and that he would be by for Marta at 7 p.m. Marta said, "How was your day Ben? How are the sales going at the department stores?"

"Fantastic!" said Ben. "Well have to increase our staff too. The stores need more merchandise. You are very good luck for me, Marta! See you later." He hurried out to James who was waiting to take him home.

Seven p.m. came all too fast for Marta, she had a lot to do to get ready. Margarite helped her get ready for the ball. She knew exactly how to comb her hair and apply the necessary make-up. Marta was wearing the light blue velvet gown. Her hair was short and combed in ringlets about her head. She wore a rope of pearls and pearl, drop earrings. Her shoes were white satin. She really looked like "The Belle of the Ball."

Ben was prompt. He looked dashing with his black tuxedo, crisp white shirt and top hat. He wore a black cape over his shoulders. He brought Marta another orchid.

"Oh, it's beautiful!" Thank you, Ben, you are so thoughtful."

"You look absolutely exquisite, Marta!" said Ben as he opened the door to let her out to the waiting car. When he helped her in, he sat down beside her and said, "I missed you so much today. I love you, Marta." Then he gathered her close to him and kissed her passionately.

Marta was looking for the sparks that she felt when Tom kissed her, but that was missing. Ben's kisses were warm and tender. She felt really good with him, but she did not have the same feeling that she had with Tom. "Maybe this will come with time," she thought to herself.

When they arrived at the Waldorf Hotel, they were ushered into the ballroom. Ben's parents were waiting for them at the door. Ben introduced Marta to them as his business partner, and dress designer. They all sat at the same table for the evening.

Ben's parents were delightful. Ben and his father excused themselves to go to the bar for drinks. While his dad had Ben alone he said, "Ben, she's beautiful I think that this is more than a business arrangement. Right?"

"Dad, I've really got it bad! I can't get her off my mind. I see her in my mind when I'm away from her. It's very painful at times. Do you think that this is love?" asked Ben.

"It sounds like it to me. She is not Jewish is she? You know that if you're thinking of marriage this could be a real problem," said his father.

"I haven't asked her to marry me, Dad, but I'm close to it I can hardly stand to be away from her. We have discussed our differences especially in religion, but not seriously. Do you have some advice for me?"

"Maybe you can have her talk to the rabbi, Ben," suggested his father.

"Well see, I'm kind of nervous even suggesting it," said Ben.

"You'll have to take it slowly, Ben. I know it's hard to do, but pray about it."

"I will. The girls will be looking for us. Let's join them," said Ben.

Meanwhile, Ben's mother was asking Marta a lot of questions. She asked about her homeland and her family. Then she asked her about her knowledge of the garment business. Marta told her that she was a novice, but her expertise was in fashion design. "I leave the rest to Ben," she said.

The men joined them with the drinks, and Marta was thankful that Ben was there to help her answer all the questions that his mother was asking her.

The orchestra was playing "Why do I love you" and Ben asked Marta to dance. They looked magnificent together. Marta began humming the tune in Ben's ear. "Can you answer that question," asked Ben.

Then the band began to play, "Moonlight and Roses." The handsome couple continued to dance. Ben felt so good dancing with Marta. She loved the way he danced and held her closely. She felt so good to Ben. He wanted to dance all evening just to hold her closely, and to feel her in his arms. She smelled like wild flowers. It was both hypnotic, and intoxicating to be near her.

When the band stopped, Ben escorted her to the table. He told his parents that he wanted to introduce Marta to some of his acquaintances. They got up and walked around to the different tables. Ben introduced Marta to a number of his friends as his business partner and dress designer. The ladies inquired about the dress that she was wearing. She told them that it was one of her designs. They asked Ben about making an appointment to talk about having clothes designed for them. He passed out his business cards when they asked for them.

After the ball was over, Mrs. Epstein asked Marta and Ben to have dinner with them on Sunday. They agreed. She asked them to come early so that they could visit before dinner.

On the way home, Ben asked Marta how she liked his parents. "I like them very much. I think that you look very much like your father. How do you think that they liked me, Ben?"

"They loved you," said Ben. "Come over closer to me, Marta, I want to put my arms around you." She accommodated, and he kissed her on the neck.

Chapter Eight

Ben came early Sunday morning to pick up Marta to take her to Connecticut to have dinner with his parents. He drove himself, because James had the day off. Marta was ready and said, "This will be the good time for you to speak to your parents about our business. I'll be so happy to get to know them better, as well."

As they entered the driveway, there was a locked gate. Ben got out and rang the bell. The butler answered and the gates opened. They drove up a long driveway to the house. It was a colonial style, very impressive. Ben got out and helped Marta. He gave her a hug as they walked up the steps to the door. The butler was already waiting for them. "Hi Charles! Let me introduce you to my friend Marta."

"I'm happy to meet you," said Marta. "Ben has told me all about you."

"I hope it's all good," said Charles, as they followed him to the library.

The library was lined with books, except for the fireplace and a large window facing a garden covered with snow. The fire was crackling in the fireplace.

Mr. and Mrs. Epstein met them as they entered the room and gave each of them a hug. "How was your trip? You made very good time," said Mr. Epstein.

"We had a beautiful drive. The weather is perfect today, and Ben is a very good driver," said Marta.

"Charles, will you bring us a pot of tea and some biscuits, please?" asked Mrs. Epstein.

"I'll send it in to you right away," said Charles.

Ben and Marta sat together on the couch, and his parents sat in the chairs on each side of them. There was a coffee table in the front of them. Marta complimented them on their home. Mrs. Epstein asked if she would like to have a look around. Ben said that he would be happy to give Marta a tour later.

Then Mrs. Epstein proceeded to get a family album to show Marta. There were pictures of Ben when he was a baby, and all the way up to the present. They spent a couple of hours looking and laughing at them. Marta was very interested in seeing the family pictures.

Charles came to the door and announced that dinner was served. They went into a lovely dining room. The room had many windows. The ceiling was high. A large chandelier hung above the table. Mr. and Mrs. Epstein took the head and the foot of the table. Marta and Ben sat across from each other. The entrée was turkey, and dressing with all the trimmings. For dessert they had pumpkin pie and whipped cream.

They chatted all during the dinner. Mr. Epstein was asking about the business. Ben was happy to reply that the fashions that were all of the same design went over very big in the department stores. Then they told them about the ladies at the ballet who wanted individual designs just for themselves. And that they did not want to see the same dress on someone else. Then Mrs. Epstein said, "I can relate to that. Now, you'll have to ask for a higher price, won't you, Ben?"

"Absolutely," said Ben. "We haven't come into an agreement as to how much yet, we'll have to discuss this, Marta. Do you have any ideas, Dad?"

"You'll have to check on the going prices for this, and also to think of the time that you will have to spend with each customer," said Mr. Epstein. "It sounds like you and Marta are going great with your business. Mother and I will have to come over to see your operation one of these days."

"By all means, you know that you are welcome. We're really busy with the holiday gowns and dresses. We have a lot of good help. Any time will be fine. Just give me a call," said Ben. "I need to walk off some of this delicious food, why don't I take Marta around and show her the place."

Ben took Marta by the arm and began to show her the living room, kitchen, and up the winding stairs to the rooms upstairs. He showed her his parents' bedroom. When they entered, Marta was amazed at the size of the room. It had a fireplace too. They had a huge bed. Ben gave Marta a hug and kissed her. "I just had to get you alone, so that I could do that," said Ben. His parents had a sitting room off their bedroom.

They had five bedrooms upstairs, and three bathrooms. It was so "homey" even though it was very exquisite. The colors were in pastels. Marta knew that if she married Ben, she would have a beautiful home too. They went downstairs to join his parents.

"It's getting late, we'll have to leave before it gets dark," said Ben as he gave his parents a big hug." Thanks for the wonderful dinner and visit."

Marta went over and thanked them both for the delicious dinner and delightful visit. Then she hugged them both. "I especially enjoyed the family pictures, for sure the one of Ben in the buff when he was six months old," teased Marta.

Mrs. Epstein said, "I'm glad that you enjoyed that picture. It's very special to me too. We'll have to do this again, real soon."

"Don't forget to give me a call when you are planning to come into town to see our business operation. You can give me some very good suggestions, dad," said Ben.

"We'll call you about Thursday to see if it is a good time to visit you," said Dad as they waved goodbye to the two lovebirds.

After leaving the grounds and they were on their way home, Ben motioned for Marta to sit closer to him. She did this, happily. They were quiet for a time. It was so nice to be together. It felt so right and comfortable.

Ben said, "I want to show you my home. It's on Long Island. It needs your warm touch, Marta. Maybe we can do that next Sunday, Okay?"

"That sounds great, Ben! I don't have anything planned. We can leave early and spend the day like we did today," said Marta.

Ben walked her to the door, and held her closely as he kissed her tenderly. Then he opened the door. What a surprise Marta had! There was Tom waiting for her. "Tom, what a surprise! Let me introduce you to Ben, my business partner. He's the gentleman who attended the fashion show on the ship, and he gave me his business card?"

"Oh, yes, I do remember. It's nice to see you again. Have you been working today?" questioned Tom.

"Oh, no," said Ben. "We drove out to Connecticut to visit with my parents. My father was also in the garment business. He's retired now, but I do like to talk over business with him. He did give us some good suggestions."

"Yes," said Marta, "I met them at the holiday ball, and they invited us for dinner today."

"I'll see you in the morning, Marta; we have a lot of holiday business to take care of. It's good to see you again, Anna and John. Let's get together during the holidays." Then he walked out the door and waved goodbye to everyone.

Marta sat on a chair next to her Aunt. Tom seemed a bit annoyed with the situation. "I want to hear about your work, Tom," said Marta.

"I'm working for the Marquette Lines," said Tom. "It's hard work. I'm a switchman now, but there is potential. I can work my way up. Tell me about your work, Marta."

"I'm doing exactly what I want to do. I'm a dress designer. Ben is making twenty dresses to one of my designs and marketing them in the department stores. We are serving six department stores and the sales are going fast. I also help Uncle John and Aunt Anna," answered Marta.

"Uncle John was telling me all about the excitement of the White Slavery Ring. I'm so glad that no one was hurt and that you were able to rescue some of the girls. Did they finally break up the ring?" asked Tom.

"Not completely," said Uncle John. "Several of the gangsters were caught, but there are still many out there who either escaped or disappeared. The police are still working on this. We'll talk about this tomorrow. Anna and I will say goodnight. You two young people would like a little time alone.

You can sleep in the sewing room, Tom. Margarite and Sofia have moved out. Inga is still out on her date with Matt. They should be along soon. Goodnight Tom and Marta don't stay up too late. It's work tomorrow. Tom, how would like to help us in the store tomorrow? We could sure use you."

"I'd like to help," said Tom.

After they were alone, Tom asked Marta to join him on the couch. She obliged. He wanted to put his arm around her, but Marta declined. "Tom, I don't want to get serious about anyone. I have my career to think about."

"I want to kiss you and hold you again. I've missed you so much, Marta," said Tom.

"It's nice to see you, again, Tom, okay, just for old times sake."

"Did you feel the electricity?" asked Tom.

"Yes, I did," said Marta, "But that doesn't make a good marriage. Passion passes soon after you're married - so my aunt says."

"What do you mean?" asked Tom.

"You need more than passion - you need common interests. We'll talk more about this in the morning. I'm exhausted! I've had a long day. I'll see you at breakfast."

Tom was surprised at the change in Marta. He would have to take a different approach to win her over. He tossed and turned as he tried to sleep.

Marta thought about what had transpired. She knew what she wanted to do, and it did not include Tom. Ben and Tom were as different as night and day. She could see a future with Ben, because of their common interests. She also tossed and turned until the wee hours in the morning. What a dilemma! She could find security and kindness with Ben, and possibly face poverty and a lot of passion with Tom. Which way should she go? There was another problem, religion. Tom was Lutheran, the same as she was, and Ben was Jewish. She soon fell asleep.

Everyone was bustling about getting ready for work. Inga looked very tired. She and Matt were out very late. Marta looked tired, because she had trouble sleeping. Tom looked haggard, because of his lack of sleep. Aunt Anna and Uncle John looked very rested.

"You got in kind of late, Inga," said Aunt Anna.

"Yes, I did. Matt and I had a lot to discuss. We plan on getting married on Valentine's Day. We are trying to decide whether to have a church wedding or just eloping. We have another problem. Matt is Catholic and I am Lutheran. I know that my parents would be against this marriage for that reason. We love each other so much that we are trying to work things out. We're both Christians. We both believe in Christ. Matt is dead set on raising the children Catholic. I think they should have the benefit of both churches, and when they grow up, they can choose. Matt doesn't believe in this. I'll have to convince him of having both churches.

"Do you think that you will continue working?" asked Aunt Anna.

"Oh, yes, I will work until I become pregnant," said Inga.

"Here is Tom," said Marta. "Tom, I want you to meet Inga. She works at the shop with us. She does beautiful embroidery on our fashions."

"How do you do?" said Tom. "It sounds like you are very talented."

"Inga, getting back to your problem, we'll have to discuss this further. This is a very serious problem. I think that the best thing for you to do is to talk to the minister of the church. I will invite the Reverend for dinner. You and Matt can come and ask all the questions that you have concerning the Lutheran Church. I think that you will find that there are not that many differences," said Aunt Anna.

"Thank you, Aunt Anna, I'll talk it over with Matt when he picks me up for lunch today."

"Tom, you're going to help us today," said Uncle John. "I can really use your artistic touch with these Christmas wreaths and center pieces."

After breakfast, they all set out for work. Marta was picked up by James. The rest of the people walked. It was a brisk morning, and it felt good to stretch their legs. When Marta and James arrived at the factory, Ben was waiting for them. He asked

Marta to step into his office after she removed her coat and boots.

"Did you have a nice evening? Isn't Tom the gentleman who was pursuing you on the ship?" asked Ben.

"Yes, to both questions," replied Marta. "Tom is a good friend, that's all. I have no intentions in getting serious with him. We have nothing in common except for religion and we both have a Finnish background."

"Marta, I do love you. We have to discuss the religious part, I know. I just don't know quite how to do this. Would you be interested in talking to the rabbi with me? Would be difficult for you?" asked Ben.

"Only if you would talk with my minister, you could ask all the questions that you may have been wondering about."

"That's a promise, Marta. I'll ask Mother and Dad to invite a rabbi over to dinner. Then you can ask him all the questions that you have in mind. Then I will meet with your minister. Is that a deal?"

"As a matter of fact, Inga and Matt are planning on marrying on Valentine's Day. They have a problem with religion too. Matt is Catholic and Inga is Lutheran. Aunt Anna has invited the minister of the Lutheran church to come to dinner to speak to them. Would you like to come at that time, Ben?"

"I would prefer to meet with the minister at a different time. Make an appointment with him. As you know, my questions will be much different from that of Matt's. Why don't we wait until after the holidays? What do you say about that, Marta?" asked Ben.

Then Ben walked over to her and took her into his arms. She really loved to be close to Ben, but she did not have the same electricity that she has with Tom.

"Will you marry me, if we get everything resolved with the religious part?" asked Ben hopefully.

"Of course I will think about it. We have so much in common. We could have a lot of fun enjoying music, art and our business. I know that you will make a good father, Ben."

He agreed and then let her go to her office where she worked diligently. She got several more fashions drafted, also a cape and a coat. Her day fashions were getting shorter each day. The women loved the freedom that they found with the shorter styles.

Chapter Nine

At noon, Marta said goodbye to Ben and went off to Uncle John's store. Tom was there to greet her. He showed Marta what he had been doing to help Uncle John. He was very artistic. When Matt came in to pick up Inga for lunch, Marta introduced Tom to him. Matt suggested that they all go to a place where young people dance. Tom and Marta agreed to go out with them. Marta wanted to see what the young people were wearing. She also wanted to show Tom a good time while he was in New York.

That evening, Tom and Marta joined Inga and Matt for a swing around town. They found a little restaurant with a live band. They were fascinated with the new dance called the "Charleston" and were joining in the dance. They learned quickly. What fun they had whirling about. They laughed and carried on all evening - not missing a step.

As they drove home, everyone was commenting on the new music and the short styles that the girls were wearing. Marta was sure that she could design a dress that would be both attractive and comfortable for this dancing craze.

Tom decided to take things much easier. He didn't want to rush Marta into anything. He waved good night to her, as she walked up the stairs to her room. He felt that he could fall asleep much easier, because he was so tired from the fast dancing.

The next day at work, Marta was anxious to share what she discovered the night before with Ben. "Matt took us out to a place where the young people were dancing. They were all having so much fun dancing the Charleston. Have you ever danced this? Let me show you how it's done," said Marta. She grabbed Ben and showed him the dance.

Ben laughed, 'Did Tom go too?"

"Yes, he did. He really enjoyed the dance too," said Marta. "I noticed that the girls needed more freedom of movement for this dance. I think that I can come up with something for this dance."

She quickly went to her office and draft table where she designed a dress that had a lot of fullness and fringes in the skirt. Then she ran across to Ben's office to show the new design.

"Hey, I think that you have another winner. Let's produce the dress. How long is Tom visiting?"

"I think that he is planning on leaving on Saturday, because he has to return to work. Don't worry - we're just good friends."

The week went by fast. Tom decided to leave on Saturday, because he had to work on Christmas day. He invited Marta to visit him in Michigan. She said that maybe she would be able to visit in the spring.

On Sunday, Ben picked her up to take her to his home on Long Island. It was a beautiful day. The sun was shining and the air was crisp. When they came to his home, the butler let them into the exquisite foyer. The floors were marble. As they walked into the living room, Marta noticed the high ceilings, which looked out to the ocean. The scenery was breathtaking. "How do you like it?" asked Ben.

"Oh I love it," said Marta. "You have done a beautiful job of decorating. Everything is done in such good taste. Let me see the rest of the house."

"This is Julian, my butler," said Ben. "Julian, this is Marta, my very good friend and business associate. We'll have dinner in about an hour. Will you bring us some tea and cookies in library, please?"

"I'll set up a table in the library, while you're showing Marta the place, and tell the cook that you'll be ready for dinner in about an hour, o.k.?"

"Let me show you the upstairs, first," said Ben. He took her by the arm and they went up the winding stairs. "This is my room." the room was very large with a lot of windows facing the ocean, with two comfortable chairs facing the windows. There was a large king size bed, dresser and everything else that would be needed for comfort. The fireplace was opposite from the windows. The bathroom was as large as Aunt Anna's living room. It had a huge tub (just right for two), a shower and sink with a dressing table. "Can you see yourself living here with me?" asked Ben.

"It would be wonderful. I can think of something that is missing. Can you guess?" asked Marta.

He took her into his arms, hugged her and whispered, while he was kissing her on the neck, "Children, darling - how many?"

Marta knew that she would have to be strong to keep things on the up and up. She moved away from him and said, "I think that two would be a good number, don't you?"

Then Ben showed her the other two bedrooms. "This will do for a while, until our family gets too large. I really want a large family. There were only two children in my family, I really would like more than that." They went down the steps to the library where Julian was ready to pour the tea.

Marta, let's discuss our problems. What if we get married and have both a Christian and Jewish home? I don't want to lose you over religion. Even though it is important to both of us. You don't have to convert to the Jewish faith. Can't we bring up our children to know both religions, and when they are older, they can decide for themselves? What do you think of this idea, Sweetheart?"

"What about the wedding, Ben? Would it be possible to have a Christian and a Jewish wedding? I want a wedding that we can invite my family along with yours."

"Oh, my darling, we'll do whatever is important to you. If you want a Christian wedding, fine, we will have that. Do you think that we could have a Jewish reception?"

"Well, that's settled! That wasn't so hard, was it? Now let's pick a date," said Ben as he walked to his desk for find a calendar. "I can't wait much longer. I miss you so much when you go home at the end of the day. I dream of you all night, when I can fall asleep." Then he took out a box from his pocket, presented a beautiful large tiffany diamond, and placed it on her left ring finger. He pulled her to him and held her in a long passionate kiss.

"We can't get married in January. I think that it would be too soon to get everything ready. February is out, because Matt and Inga are getting married on Valentine's Day," said Marta.

"What's wrong with January? We still have one week left on December. What about the middle of January? I can't wait much longer than that, Sweetheart. I want you as soon as I can have you. I know I'm being selfish, but I can't help it," said Ben.

There was a knock on the door. It was Julian announcing that dinner had been served. "We'll be right there," answered Ben. "Well, what do you say, Marta?"

"Okay, we'll try for the middle of January." Marta said reluctantly.

"You have made me the happiest man in the world. I promise you that you will not want for anything. I will spend my life making you feel safe and happy," said Ben as they walked into the dining room. The sun was setting and the sky was lit up in bright orange and yellow lights. Everything seemed bright just right for the two people in love who had found each other. When you're in love, everything looks rosy.

They talked of the wedding, who they would invite, and ordering invitations. Ben said that he would give her the money to send to her parents to come to live in America. He said that they could stay with them until they find a home of their own.

Chapter Ten

Marta sat very close to Ben all the way home. When they got there, they both went in to tell them the exciting news. "Do you think that you'll have time to get ready for the wedding?" asked Aunt Anna.

"We'll make time," said Ben. "We can get busy with the plans right away. Meanwhile, Marta can send for her parents and her brothers."

"Whatever you say," said Uncle John. "Have you told your parents about this blessed event, Ben?"

"No I haven't told them yet. They won't be surprised. They have already met Marta, and they like her a lot. They plan to visit us at the plant tomorrow. We can tell them at that time."

Ben said goodnight to Aunt Anna and Uncle John as he started for the door. Marta walked him to the car. They held each other in a long embrace. Marta whispered, "I'm going to miss you too, darling. It won't be long now. I want you too, Ben, but we must wait until we're married."

Ben said, "It better be soon, Marta, I'm in pain. I love you so much, and I have so much respect for you that I can wait. Just hold me close and promise me that you won't change the date to a later time."

"I'll write to my parents and get the check out to them. What if your parents object to our marriage, Ben?"

"I can explain everything to them. They will see things my way, I know. They only want our happiness. My mother will help with the wedding plans, Marta." Then he began nibbling at her ears and neck. Marta pulled away and said goodnight. Someone had to be strong, and she knew that it had to be herself.

She turned at the door and waved to Ben as he drove off. She went upstairs to write to her parents. As she was writing, Inga came in crying. "What's wrong, Inga?" She went over to her and put her arms around Inga.

"Matt and I are so in love, Marta. We have gone all the way, and now I'm pregnant. The wedding isn't until February. I'm afraid to tell Matt. What am I going to do?"

The next day when Matt picked up Inga for lunch, he seemed very happy and excited. When he had her alone, he asked her if she could hurry up the wedding, because he was going to be very busy in January. His boss told him that he could take off two weeks between the holidays. Inga was delighted, because then she would be married soon. When Matt stopped the car, he gathered Inga in his arms and asked her whether she could manage to have the wedding in one week.

Inga said, "Of course I can, Matt. I'm happy that you want to get married sooner. We won't have a large wedding. Let's go and talk to your mother and father about the wedding. There is something else that I want to tell you, Matt."

"What is that, my sweets?" He asked as he was nibbling at her ear.

"Matt, we're going to have a baby. I have missed my period, and I have been having morning sickness."

"Are you sure? Let's hurry and talk to my parents about the wedding. I'm really happy about the baby, Inga. The sooner we're married, the happier I'll be."

They drove off to the little restaurant that his parents operated. They rushed in to talk to his parents. They were cautious, at first, telling them not to rush into things. Then Matt told them that Inga was pregnant. They immediately agreed to the wedding. They liked Inga, and knew that Matt was in love with her. In fact, they were both in love with each other. They planned to have the wedding in the little church only a block from their restaurant. The priest was having dinner at their restaurant, and they walked over to him.

"Father, we would like to get married on Saturday morning, and we would like you to marry us," said Matt.

The priest answered, "I'll be happy to marry you. Will you have a large wedding or will you have only a few friends?"

"We plan to have a few friends, and my parents," said Matt. "Would ten in the morning be all right with you?"

"Yes, that will be fine; however, I want to have a talk with both of you, before the wedding. Can you make it to the church at 7 p.m. this evening?"

"Is that all right with you, Inga?" asked Matt.

Inga nodded her head in agreement. They both shook hands with the priest, and waved goodbye to Matt's parents.

When they got into the car, they talked about who they would invite. Also, they discussed where they would live. They will have a busy time of it. Matt kissed Inga as he dropped her off at the shop. He said, "I love you, Inga. You have made me very happy. I will do my best to make you happy. I will take care of you and the baby."

Inga was excited when she entered the shop. She told everyone that they were invited to her wedding which would be on the following Saturday at 10 a.m. They talked about making her a wedding gown. They were busy planning everything when Aunt Anna and Uncle John came in to hear the news. Everyone was happy for her.

That evening after dinner, Inga was waiting for Matt to come for her. They had an appointment at 7 p.m. with the Father. It was now 8 p.m., and Inga was pacing the floor. "What could have happened?" There was a knock on the door. Uncle John answered it. There was a police officer at the door. He had some bad news. Matt had been shot, and was in the hospital. Inga ran for her coat and asked the police officer if he would give her a ride to the hospital. He was in the emergency room, unconscious. Inga saw the priest and his parents at his side. The doctor said that he would have to have emergency surgery. He had been shot in the chest near his heart. Inga asked if she could see him, but was not permitted to do this, because of the emergency of the surgery. He was rushed to the operating room, and was in surgery for two hours. The doctor came out of surgery, and said, "All we can do now is to pray for him. I was able to remove the bullet, but he is very weak, and still unconscious. You had better go home now, and we'll call you in the morning."

Matt's parents would not leave the hospital nor would Inga. Just in case he came out of his unconsciousness, they wanted to be there. The nurses were notified to inform them as soon as they had noticed that he had gained consciousness. Inga was crying. The events of the evening were too much for her. Matt's parents both went to her and held her. Matt's mother was crying too. The priest came to them and asked them to come with him for prayer. They found a room that was empty and the Father led them in prayer for the healing power of God to permit Matt to stay with them on earth, but that God should have his way. After the prayer, the priest noticed how pale and weak Inga looked so he suggested that he take her home. Matt's father said that he would rather have the Father stay with his wife just in case that be would need to give Matt the Last Rights. Inga would not have any one of them take her home. She wanted to stay with Matt. If he was in danger of losing his life, she wanted to be near to see him once again and to whisper to him that she loved him. Also, that he needed to get well for her and her baby.

Aunt Anna and Uncle John were worried about Inga and Matt. Finally, Uncle John decided to call a cab and go down to the hospital to check on things. Aunt Anna wanted to go with him so that she could be with Inga. Marta was concerned too, they called a cab and they all went to the hospital. They soon found Matt's parents, the priest and Inga huddled together down at the far end of the hall. They were shocked to hear about Matt's condition.

The nurse motioned for the priest to come to talk to her. She said, Matt is conscious and is calling for Inga and the priest. The doctor came running too. Inga and the priest were at his side. The doctor was taking his vital signs. His heartbeat was irregular. He had a fever. Inga went to him and kissed him on the cheek. He recognized her. Then he whispered for the priest to come to him. He said that he had one request. I don't know whether I will make it so please, will you do me the favor of marrying Inga and me?

The priest said that he can get well first, but Matt would not have any part of that. Then he explained to the father that he and Inga were going to have a baby and it was very important that they were married. Then the Father understood. He asked the doctor if they could do this. The doctor said that it would be all right. So they asked Matt's parents Uncle John, Aunt Anna and Marta to join them while the priest married them. Then the doctor asked everyone to leave the room, because he needed to work on Matt's problem. By that time when everyone left the room, the ladies were all crying. The men tried to look strong, but they had tears running down their cheeks as well. After about half an hour, the doctor called in the priest to perform the Last Rights. The doctor told the family that he was failing fast. He gave Inga the first five minutes to say goodbye, then he had his parents come into the room. Matt asked his mother and father if they would take care of Inga and the baby. They assured him that they would. They also said that she could move into their home and stay in his room.

Chapter Eleven

Instead of having a wedding on Saturday, there was a gathering at the church for the funeral of Matt, Inga's beloved. It was very impressive, because there were several of the New York Police Department present who also participated in the funeral service. Everyone had something nice to say about Matt. The Police Chief spoke to Inga and Matt's parents about the possibility of one of the gangsters who was involved with the White Slavery Ring shooting Matt when he least expected it. After all, Matt was very involved in this case. He also assured them that they were doing everything possible to capture him.

Inga was grief stricken. She had difficulty eating, or sleeping. All she could think of was the loss of Matt. Aunt Anna called her into the kitchen to talk to her. She told her that she had to take care of herself because of the baby that she was carrying. She told her that she was carrying his child, who was a part of him, that this should be a comfort to her.

Inga decided to stay on with Aunt Anna, Uncle John and Marta for a while. She felt like they were family, and that she would be more comfortable with them. Matt's parents said that she was always welcome to come to live with them, but they understood that she needed her friends at this time.

They wanted her to keep in touch, and that she was welcome to come to the restaurant to eat at any time.

Marta was shaken by the events. She spoke to Ben about all that had happened. He was very understanding. He was interested in keeping the wedding date and plans early. They had to wait to hear from her parents. The day finally came; Marta received a letter from her parents. They sent the check back, because they could not accept a gift like that from Ben. They said that they had arranged to enter the United States through Canada, and that they had enough money to pay their own way. They asked her not to rush into a marriage. They wanted to talk to her about the wedding after they arrive in the Upper Peninsula of Michigan. Marta's mother had another sister who lived up there. They planned to be there in one month.

Ben was very unhappy with the news, but he knew that if he were to get along with his in-laws he would have to wait until all was settled.

Chapter Twelve

Marta was determined not to let herself get into a compromising position with Ben, especially after what happened to Inga.

It was the week before Christmas. Ben had invited Marta to the Hanukah celebration, and she in turn, invited him to the Christian celebrations of Christmas. Marta really enjoyed the menorah. She thought that it was great fun to light a candle each night before Hanukah and receive a gift each night. She thought that this would be great fun for the children.

Ben thought that it would be great fun to receive gifts on Christmas morning. The presents are to remind them of the gifts the wise men brought to the Christ child.

Ben was open to the teaching of the Christian faith. Marta was praying for him. She was praying that he would receive Christ as his personal Savior. She did this in the quietness of her room.

On Christmas Eve, Ben accompanied Marta to the church where they listened to Handel's "Messiah." The soprano sang, "And they were in the same country, shepherds abiding in the field keeping watch over their flock by night. And behold, the Angel of the Lord came upon them, and the glory of the Lord shown round about them. And they were so afraid. And the Angel said unto them, 'Fear not, for behold I bring you good tidings of great joy which shall be to all people. For unto you is born this day in the city of David, a Savior, which is Christ the Lord. And this shall be a sign unto you, ye shall find the babe wrapped in swaddling clothes, lying in a manger.' And suddenly there was with the Angel, a multitude of the Heavenly Host praising God and saying, 'Glory to God, Glory to God, Glory to God in the highest, and peace on earth. Good will toward men.' And when the angels were gone away from them into Heaven. The shepherds said one to another, 'Let us now go even unto Bethlehem and see this thing that has come to past, which the Lord hath made known unto us.' And they came with haste and found Mary, Joseph and the Babe, lying in the manger."

Ben looked at Marta with tears in his eyes. He said that he was so touched with the music and the words from the New Testament. After the concert, Ben drove Marta home, where they prayed together. The Holy Spirit was with them, and when Ben prayed, he asked that God would open his eyes and show him the path to take. Marta looked into his eyes, and said, "Ben, all you have to do is to believe that Jesus is your Messiah, and ask Him to come into your heart and life, and He will do that."

"Give me time, Marta. There are so many questions that I need answered. If Jesus is truly the Messiah that the Jewish people have been looking for, then I want to know Him. I am asking God to show me the way to take. I am open, Marta, just have patience with me, okay?"

Then Marta and Ben held each other and kissed each other goodnight. Marta asked Ben to join her and the family for Christmas. She said, "Try to be here early, like around ten, because we like to open our gifts the first thing in the morning. When we were children we awakened before dawn to find out what Santa had delivered."

Ben agreed to do this. He was planning to stay at the Waldorf Hotel so that he would not have to travel that far. They said goodbye and hurried off.

The next morning, Aunt Anna and Uncle John were busy getting ready for the Christmas dinner. The turkey and dressing was in the oven. The aroma was really tantalizing. Aunt Anna was rolling out the pie dough. Uncle John was busy peeling the potatoes. Inga was making the cranberry sauce, and Marta was making the snowflake pudding.

There was a knock on the door. Uncle John answered it, and to his surprise, it was his daughter Helen and her husband Anker. Aunt Anna heard the commotion and went into the living room to find out what was the matter. They were all talking at once when Marta introduced Inga. They all went into the living room as Anker went out to the car to bring in their gifts.

There was another knock at the door, and this time Marta answered it. Of course, there was Ben, waiting for his Christmas hug and kiss. The mistletoe was just above the door, and they really took advantage of it. She pulled him into the living room, and introduced everyone to him. Ben placed his gifts under the tree and joined Marta on the sofa. Aunt Anna and Inga served coffee and delicious apple strudel that they had prepared. She said, "I put an almond into one of the pastries. The person who finds it gets to open the first gift."

"Oh," said Ben, "I just found the almond. It looks like I'm the lucky one." Marta passed a gift to him from under the tree. It was a small package from Marta. He opened it to find a beautiful pair of gold cufflinks with his initials on them. He was thrilled with the gift, and gave Marta a kiss on the cheek as he thanked her.

Marta was next. She found an oblong box from Ben. She opened it to find a stunning gold bracelet with diamonds. They all ooed and awed over it. She went to Ben, embraced him, and thanked him for the gift. He helped her put the bracelet on. She lifted up her arm to admire it and loved moving her wrist so that she could see the diamonds sparkle.

There was a gift for everyone from Ben. He brought Aunt Anna a beautiful brooch. He gave Uncle John a tool kit. Inga received a silk scarf. He also brought a large box of See's candy for the family to share.

Uncle John made jewelry boxes for everyone. He carved their names on them, and lined them with red velvet. They told him that they would cherish his gift to them. Even the men enjoyed their boxes.

Aunt Anna knit sweaters for everyone. A pink one for Inga, a light green one for Marta, a red one for Ben, a white one, for Uncle John and Anker, and a light blue one for Helen. They were both practical and lovely. They all thanked her for the gifts.

Inga crocheted gloves for everyone, and Marta knitted a scarf for them. Helen and Anker brought fresh oranges and avocados from California. They also brought macadamia nuts that were new to them. The nutshells were so hard, that they had to bring a special nutcracker. The avocados were new to them also. Helen made a dip from them and spiced it with onions, garlic and lemon.

Marta went to the piano, and began playing Christmas carols. They all joined in and sang while Aunt Anna and Uncle John went to the kitchen to check on the turkey.

Soon everything was placed on the table and they all sat around. Aunt Anna had used her finest china and linens for this special occasion. In the center of the table, was one of Uncle John's masterpieces. His design was made of spruce, pine and decorated with red holly berries. In the center was a red candle, which they lit. You could smell the fresh pine.

Uncle John sat at the head of the table. He asked everyone to bow their head as he thanked the Lord for the blessings that they had bestowed upon them. He also thanked God for His bountiful gifts of food and for the safety of his family and friends. Then he began carving the delicious turkey. It was juicy and tender. In fact, it was difficult to cut, because of it. The dressing smelled so good - you could smell the cornbread, onions, sage and other spices. The aroma was very inviting to the hungry pallet. Aunt Anna served the mashed potatoes, gravy, creamed carrots, buttered asparagus, cranberries and apple - pecan salad. Soon it was time for dessert. Everyone said that they would rather wait until later.

The men decided to go for a walk, while the ladies busied themselves in the kitchen. When the men finally returned, the ladies had the dessert and coffee ready on the table. They served, pumpkin, mincemeat and pecan pies.

Ben said, "This has been a great Christmas for me. Thank you for the lovely gifts, delicious food, and great company. Now, I have to leave and visit with my family. My sister, her husband and children are here from California. I want them to meet Marta.

Marta went upstairs to get her coat, and purse. She also fixed her hair and primped up a bit. When she returned, she gave everyone a hug and said that she would be back later in the evening.

As they drove off, it began to snow. It was gently falling. Marta snuggled next to Ben. It was cozy, being together. It took an hour to reach his parents' house. The butler met them at the door, and took their coats, boots and hats. Then he escorted them to the living room. Everyone was happy to see them. They had been worried about them because of the storm. Ben introduced his sister, her husband and their two children to Marta as his fiancée.

"When's the big event?" asked Ruth.

"Soon, I hope," answered Ben. "We're waiting to hear from Marta's parents."

Just then the children came running to Ben, "Uncle Ben, come and show us how to put our train together. We got it for Hanukah." They pulled on him to come.

"Marta, this is Sara and Joshua, my niece and nephew," said Ben.

"Hi!" they both said. "You can come to help us put the train together too." They followed the children to the library where the train was to be set up. The children gathered the tracks and handed them to Ben. As he was putting the pieces together, Marta could see how much he enjoyed his niece and nephew. "He'll make a good father," thought Marta.

The children ran to tell their parents and grandparents to come to the library and watch the train go around. They had a Hanukah bush that looked very much like a Christmas tree.

At six o'clock, the butler announced dinner. Marta and Ben were still stuffed from lunch, but they managed. Ben's father asked them to bow their head and thank God for His bountiful blessings much the same way as Uncle John had; however, Jesus, our Lord was never mentioned.

The dinner was delicious. They were served Cornish hens, dressing, with all the trimmings. They had the servants wait on them. When the dinner was finished, they didn't have to help clean. Marta was thankful for that, because she was tired from helping at Aunt Anna's.

After dinner, Ben wanted to be alone with Marta. He wanted to hold her and to talk of their future. They sat down in the living room where the fire was crackling. They looked through the large window and noticed that the snow was coming down fast. They would not be able to drive home tonight. They were snowbound. Ben's mother came into the room and said, "Ben, you and Marta must stay with us tonight. I don't want you to drive in this frightful storm."

"That's what I was telling Marta," said Ben." You call Aunt Anna and Uncle Ben that you will be staying with my parents.

"Yes, I'll do that," answered Marta.

"Let me talk to her too," said Mrs. Epstein. "I'll assure her that you are well chaperoned, and will be safer here than in the storm."

So they went to the phone. When they talked to Aunt Anna, she had agreed that it would be too dangerous to try to drive back.

Then Ben and Marta resumed their plans in the living room, while Mrs. Epstein was getting the sleeping arrangements ready.

Ben said, "Marta, do you think that we could get married before your parents come from Finland?"

Marta answered, "Yes, if you will agree to have a Christian wedding."

Ben thought for a while, "I'll agree to that if we can have some of the Jewish traditions during the reception."

Marta agreed to that. "Then let's make a date. We'll have a small wedding and the reception at the Waldorf. I am planning to close the factory for two weeks while we're on our honeymoon, or maybe dad would like to supervise while we're gone. I'll ask him," said Ben.

"Where will we go on our honeymoon?"

"How would you like to take the train down to Florida, where it is nice and warm?" asked Ben.

"I'd love to go down there to warm up!" exclaimed Marta.

"Then it's settled. How about getting married on New Year's Day?"

"If we can make all the arrangements in such short notice. I'll ask your sister to be my matron of honor, and Inga can be the bridesmaid. Maybe you can ask your brother-in-law to be your best man?" "I'll make the arrangements for the traditional mazel tov for the reception. I'll ask my mother to help with the plans. Marta, you've made me the happiest man in the world." He explained after he pulled her over to him and kissed her passionately.

Just then, Ben's mother came into the living room to tell them of the sleeping arrangements. Ben announced that the wedding was to be on January 1st, and that he would like to have it early so that his sister and her family can also be in the wedding, besides a few other things.

"I know what the other things are" teased his mother, "but right now I want to tell Marta about the sleeping arrangements. Marta, you will be sleeping in the pink guest room to the right, at the top of the stairs. Ben, you will sleep in your own room at the end of the hall. I have placed a nightgown and fresh towels on the bed, Marta. Now that we have settled that please join us in the library so that we can make plans for the nuptials."

They went to the library and found the children in their pajamas saying goodnight to everyone. They jumped up in Ben's arms, gave him a hug, and kissed Marta. They begged for a story. Their dad said, "Come now, I have a story for you." They went off to bed.

"We have set a date for our wedding," announced Ben, "We're going to be married on January 1st."

"Next week?" asked Mr. Epstein. "That's Ben, for you, always thinking ahead."

"Yes, Dad, we love each other and want to be together," replied Ben. "We're having a small wedding, just for the family and for a few close friends."

"Have you resolved your religious differences?" asked Mrs. Epstein. "Problems like this can blow up, after the honeymoon is over."

"Yes, to a certain extent," replied Ben. "We'll have a Christian wedding service, but we'll have a Jewish reception."

"Well, that's interesting, but what about afterwards? What about rearing the children?" asked Mr. Epstein.

"We have been comparing both religions, and have found truths that we can accept in both; however, I know that Marta will never accept the fact that Christ is not the Messiah. She is a strong believer that Jesus Christ is the Messiah that we have been waiting for. We pray together, and I can feel the presence of the Lord as we pray. Now we are studying the New Testament together. I'm open - I want to know all there is to know," said Ben.

"Well, that's well and good, but don't lose the Jewish faith," said his father.

"There are many traditions in the Jewish faith that I will keep, but I'm also open to the Christian faith," said Ben openly, "Meanwhile, let's do some planning for the big event. We plan to have about thirty people attend the wedding, and the reception at the Waldorf Hotel. They have a wedding chapel in the hotel; we can be married there. Marta is going to find a minister to marry us. Mother and Dad, you will have to help me with the reception. We want Ruth to be the matron of honor and Joseph to be the best man, Joshua, can be the ring bearer and Sarah to be the flower girl."

Ben's mother started writing down everything. "We won't have time to send out invitations. We'll have to call the people on the phone. Ben, are you sure you want to rush things like this?"

"Yes, I do, because Marta's cousin and her husband are here from California, as well as Ruth and Joseph. It's also a good time, because after the holidays, business is a little slow. I can close the factory for two weeks, or maybe Dad can supervise while I'm gone."

"I think that it would be good to close down, your employees will appreciate a vacation," said Mr. Epstein.

Marta was thinking of all the things that she would have to do before the wedding, including a dress to wear. She knew that she could count on Aunt Anna and Inga to help.

"Let's go to bed now, and let our love birds have a few minutes to themselves," said Ben's mom. They said good night as they left the room.

The Butler peeked in to say goodnight. He asked if they would like some hot chocolate and cookies before they went off to bed. They both said, "Please do bring us some." A few minutes later, they were served. Ben got up and poked around in the fire and laid on another log. It was such a cozy feeling. It was storming outside and they were warm, in front of the fire snuggling together, as they drank their hot chocolate and munched on their cookies.

"Ben, I don't know anything about sex. My mother just told me that it was important not to have that until after marriage. She also said that it was a natural occurrence when too people are in love. I know that is how babies are born, but I don't know how to have sex and prevent the babies. I wouldn't want to have too many babies."

Ben chuckled and said, "Leave that up to me, darling. There are ways to prevent having babies, but I don't want to prevent them until it is necessary. I want to have a family soon, after all, I'm thirty years old. I want to enjoy my children while I am young. As far as sex goes, I'll teach you all there is to know. Let's begin on our honeymoon. Right now, I don't want to talk about it. It just want to kiss you and hold you."

After a long passionate kiss his hands began to move on her body when Marta stopped him. She took his hands into hers and said, "I really love it when you caress me, but I think that it will lead to other things. Let's just talk for a while. I want to tell you about some of the things that I love about you. First, I love your eyes. They are a piercing blue, and when you look into mine, I can feel that you are looking into the depth of my soul. Yet, they are warm and compassionate. I love your presence. When you walk into a room, everyone feels your presence. I love your business head. You are good at what you do and are in command. I love to watch you when you don't know that I'm watching you. Your profile is strong, and handsome. Your lips are full and demanding. I love to hear you speak. You have a full command of the English language and your voice has resonance. You know how to handle money, yet you are very generous.

Ben looked at her, "Are you sure that you are talking about me?"

"Yes, my darling, it's you and I am truly in love with you."

"Now it's my turn," said Ben. "I love the way you look. You are beautiful! "I love your auburn hair, green sparkling eyes, and creamy complexion. I respect your business mind, and your artistic designs. Even though, I want children, I want you to know that you will always be a part of the business. You will help me make all the decisions concerning our life and the business. I love the way you move, you are so feminine, even though you have the mind of a businessman. My sweetheart, you have the softest skin. I can hardly keep my hands off you, but I promised you that I would keep my distance until we are married. Then watch out! I'll probably eat you up!" Then he grabbed her and kissed her behind the ear, her neck, her face. Then they both started laughing and kissing.

"Tomorrow, we'll have to get our marriage license. Then we'll have to get everything arranged. You talk to Aunt Anna about the minister and the flowers. I suppose you will be busy with your wedding gown. I know you'll want your own design. I'll leave the wedding up to you, and I'll take care of the reception, reservations at the hotel in the bridal suite, the compartment on the train, and reservations at a resort in Miami. We might even take a ship to the Bahamas. This will be a surprise for you."

"We're going to have a busy week. I think that we had better go to sleep now. Although, I don't know how much sleep I'll get. I just want to curl up in your arms and sleep with you," said Marta.

"Don't tempt me," said Ben, as he turned out the light and started up the stairs. "This is your room, Sweetheart." He walked her into her room. It was soft and feminine, just like Marta. The bathroom was off to the right of the bed. Ben held her close, and kissed her goodnight. Then he walked out and closed the door. He was so thrilled about the wedding! Just one week away. He went to his room and tried to get some sleep. He tossed and turned and soon fell asleep.

Marta washed and hung up her undergarments and stockings in the bathroom. Then she went to sleep feeling the warmth and love that she had for Ben.

She woke up with the sun shining into the bedroom. The room felt warm. She got up to take a bath and get ready for the day. She washed her hair too. It was naturally curly so she towel dried it and brushed it out. Then she just had to push it into shape. It formed ringlets around her face. Her undergarments and stockings had dried during the night. She had some make-up in her handbag and she primped up a bit. She was wearing her Kelly green tailored suit, pleated skirt, angora white knit blouse and fitted jacket. She was wearing black paten leather shoes. Her skirt came to the mid-calf. She had beautifully shaped ankles.

She went downstairs to find Ben waiting for her. "I thought you'd never wake up. It's ten o'clock already. Let's go into the breakfast room to have something to eat." He gave her a quick hug and kissed her on the cheek. "You smell so good. Yum! I guess I'll eat you for breakfast."

"Oh Ben, you had better stop that, your family will see you kissing me. Have the roads been cleared?" asked Marta.

"Yes, I have already checked on that. It's smooth sailing right down to city hall for our marriage license. You haven't changed your mind, have you?"

"You must be joking, I'm just as anxious for this event, as you are," she exclaimed.

The Epsteins had already eaten. The children were outside building a snowman. So Marta and Ben had the room to themselves. They were served poached eggs on toast, a glass of orange juice and a cup of coffee.

Then they found the family, thanked them for their hospitality, and said their goodbyes. The children ran to them with snow-covered clothes and mittens and hugged them. They laughed when they saw the snowmen.

The Epsteins were a little concerned about the rush to have the wedding, but they knew that Ben was determined. So they made up their minds to help in any way that they could.

Ben and Marta drove right down to city hall and filed for a marriage certificate. They were informed that they needed a blood test. So Ben called his doctor. They drove to get their blood tested, and Ben asked for a rush so they could proceed with their marriage license. The doctor said they should have the results by morning.

After that, they left the doctor's office and drove over to Aunt Anna's store. Sure enough they were all there working hard, as usual. Uncle John was busy making jewelry boxes to sell in the store. He was using the tools that he got from Ben for Christmas.

They went into their back room for a talk. Marta and Ben gave everyone a big smile, and Marta said, "Ben and I have decided to get married on New Year's Day and we would like you to participate in the wedding."

"I know that your parents will be disappointed when they will not be able to attend. Have you notified them?" asked Aunt Anna.

"I know that they will understand. I wish with all my heart, that they could be here, but they can't and we don't want to wait."

"I'm disappointed," answered Aunt Anna, "I had hoped that you would wait for your parents, but I'll cooperate. What do you want us to do?"

"For starters, we want you to find a minister to marry us," said Ben. "We want a Christian wedding. Uncle John, will you give Marta away?"

"Of course, I will," said Uncle John.

"A Christian minister, ok, that should be easy," said Aunt Anna.

"I want Inga and Helen to be bridesmaids," said Marta. "I don't know how we'll get all the sewing done. That's the only thing that's worrying me."

"Don't worry about that, Darling," said Ben, "I'll get my employees to come into the factory to help. Marta, you submit the designs and we'll get the sewing done."

"See how he is," said Marta, "That's why I love him so much. He knows how to take care of everything."

"Anker, we want you to be an usher in the wedding, Okay?"

"I'll be glad to be a part of the big event," said Anker.

Marta and Ben took off to the factory to call the workers in for the next day. They were able to reach everyone. They said that they would be there the next day to begin on the dresses.

Ben called the Waldorf to see if he could reserve the chapel and a ballroom for the reception. They asked him to come by the hotel to make the necessary arrangements and to put down a deposit. So they locked up the factory, and got into their car to set off for the hotel. They went to the caterer's office. He had everything there to help. He reserved the bridal suite for January 1. They were able to reserve the chapel and grand ballroom for the reception. They even had flowers for the wedding. Ben gladly wrote a check to reserve everything. They had to decide on a menu for the reception. They decided to have the wedding at 10 a.m., and then serve lunch at the reception. They looked at the menu and decided on fruit salad, leg of lamb, mint sauce, green beans, mashed potatoes, rolls and of course the wedding cake. All of this served with coffee, tea or milk. There was no alcohol, because of prohibition.

Ben and Marta looked at the time. It was seven p.m. They had really accomplished a lot! They were famished so they decided to eat in the dining room. They sat down, and looked at each other. "Wow! We've really covered a lot of territory. I'll call my Mom and Dad tonight and tell them that we can have up to 50 guests. I know that they will want to invite my relatives and some close friends. Are you happy, darling?"

"Yes, but I'm exhausted. It will be beautiful. We want it to be something that we will remember for always. Guess what we forgot? A photographer, Ben, do you know where we can get one?"

"I knew there was something that we had forgotten. I'll ask Dad if he can suggest someone. I'll have to make reservations for the compartment on the train and the resort in Miami. I'll call from the factory in the morning. I want the resort to be a surprise for you," said Ben as he squeezed her hand and gazed into her eyes.

"Don't you think that we should invite the employees to the wedding too? After all, they will be helping with the dresses."

Chapter Thirteen

When they reached Aunt Anna and Uncle John's they were bombarded with questions. "Just a minute," said Ben, "One question at a time."

"Were you able to get the ladies in the factory to help with the sewing?" asked Aunt Anna.

"Yes, they'll help, the cutting, measuring and the sewing," said Ben.

Then Marta began explaining, "I have to sketch designs for the dresses, and take the measurements. Then they can do the cutting and sewing. I want Inga to sew in some pearls into the bodice of my gown, and also on the sleeves."

"Have you made the arrangements at the hotel?" asked Uncle John.

"Oh, yes, even the flowers have been ordered, "replied Ben, "We do have to get a photographer and some musicians for the service and the reception."

"How many people would you like to invite?" asked Marta.

"Probably about ten people," said Aunt Anna. "I'm going to call my sister in Calumet, Michigan to see whether or not she and her family can come."

"Then I'll call my parents and tell them that they can invite about thirty people," said Ben. "May I use your telephone? I need to call my chauffeur and ask him to bring some clothes for me. I plan to stay at the Waldorf tonight. I'm just too tired to drive home." Then he walked to the phone to call. "I'm going to leave now, if you have any questions, you can let Marta fill me in."

He said good evening to them and headed for the door as Marta followed. They stopped on the porch to hold each other and kiss goodnight. "It won't be long now, sweetheart," he whispered in Marta's ear and started kissing her on the neck. They said goodbye and Marta went into the living room to answer more questions. Helen and Anker were very happy to participate in the wedding. Helen would be a bridesmaid and Anker an usher. They were planning to ship out to Denmark on the third of January. Anker told Uncle John that he could use his car until they returned in six months.

Marta got her sketchpad and started sketching the dresses for the bridesmaids. She had to consider the material that was in stock and the usefulness of the dresses after the wedding. She decided on a light blue wool, floor length, scoop neckline, long sleeves, princess style. Then she had to measure everyone. Inga offered her wedding dress, because she hadn't worn it at all. Marta thanked her and told her that she should keep it. "This dress is very special to you, Inga; I can design my own and have it made for me."

Helen had a tiara that she brought with her, and offered it to Marta. She looked at it, and saw that it would work with a veil. She had some lace that she could sew on it with a train down the back. Her dress would be made of a cream-colored lace, long sleeves, high neck, fitted front, gathered with a small bustle in the back. She asked Inga if she would sew some pearls on the bodice and sleeves.

Aunt Anna needed a dress too; after all, she was acting as the "Mother of the Bride." There would be enough material left over to make her a light blue dress with a jacket to match.

It was late by the time Marta finished her designs. She was the only one still up. She and Inga gave up their room for Helen and Anker. Inga was sleeping in the sewing room, and Marta was sleeping on the sofa in the living room. Aunt Anna made up the sofa to look very comfortable. Marta was so tired that she could have slept on the floor. She crawled in between the blankets and fell right to sleep.

She woke up early, because everyone was bustling about trying to take turns in the bathroom. Aunt Anna was busy in the kitchen frying pancakes. The coffee was perking with a rich aroma and the cinnamon rolls were baking. You could smell the bacon frying. Marta quickly got up and put on her robe. She hurriedly folded up the sheets and blankets and placed them at the end of the sofa so that she could carry them upstairs later. Anker and Helen were already dressed and had gone into the kitchen drinking a cup of coffee. Marta asked if it was okay to get some of her clothes out of her room and to use the bathroom. They told her to go right in and get her clothes. She picked out a black wool suit, a pink sweater and found stockings, shoes and underwear. Then she rushed into the bathroom for a quick shower. It took her a half an hour. It was 8:30 a.m. and she was expecting Ben momentarily. Fifteen minutes later, Uncle John opened the door for Ben. He looked sharp in his pinstriped suit. Aunt Anna told him to sit down and have some breakfast. He obliged and sat next to Marta. He gave her a squeeze on the arm and kissed her on the cheek.

"You know, we may have a problem with tuxedoes, the best man and the ushers will need them," said Marta.

"Have you asked Anker? I know that Joseph has one."

"As a matter of fact, I do have one," answered Anker. "Do you want me to wear it for the wedding?"

"Yes," said Ben. "Now, we are complete."

"I have made the designs for the dresses, and I'm sure that we have enough light blue wool material," said Marta. "It will deplete our stock, but maybe we can stop in South Carolina on the way back from our honeymoon to buy more material."

"You sweet lady, you are thinking of our business even at a time like this," exclaimed Ben. "We hope to have a dress rehearsal on New Year's Eve, at about 5 p.m. After the rehearsal, everyone is invited for dinner. My parents are providing that for us."

"We should be able to try on the dresses by tomorrow and to get the hemlines correct. Be sure to wear the shoes that you are planning to wear at the fitting," said Marta. "Aunt Anna, were you able to find a minister to marry us?"

"Not yet, but that's my big job today. I'm going to call on the minister from our Lutheran Church first," she said.

"Are you ready, Marta?" Ben asked. "Let's get those designs into the factory. Inga, would you like to come along and help?"

"Oh, yes, let me get my hat and coat," said Inga.

They bundled up and set off to the garment factory. As they arrived, they could see the employees outside ready to start to work on the big project. They were so happy to help, and to be invited to the happy event. They liked both Marta and Ben.

After removing their boots, hats and coats, Marta had a meeting with the employees to explain everything to them. She laid down the designs for the maids of honor. The cutter looked at the designs and the material. She said that with measurements that she could do this. She would first cut it out on paper, and then get Marta's approval. She cut out the first pattern, Marta said that it was perfect, she started on the material. The sewers got their sewing machines ready with the right color thread.

As they were busy getting the dresses ready, Ben got his mother on the phone. Marta asked to talk to her too. She wanted to ask if the children had something special to wear for the wedding, because Sara was to be the flower girl, and Josh was to be the ring bearer. Mrs. Epstein assured her that they would take care of this. She asked what color the wedding party would be wearing. Then Ben asked about a photographer. Mr. Epstein said that he would take care of that, and not to worry.

Well, everything was moving right along. After the cutter finished with the bridesmaid's dresses and the maid of honor, she started on the wedding dress. Marta's dress was to be made of cream lace with a satin lining. By five o'clock, everything was ready for the fittings. They decided to save that for the next day. Ben called his sister and she said that she would be there at 10 a.m. the next day.

Ben was very pleased with his accomplishments. Everything was working like clockwork. He had made the reservations for the compartment on the train for January 2nd. He also was able to get reservations at the fabulous resort in Palm Beach, Florida.

Now, he needed someone to sing at the wedding and musicians for dancing at the reception. "Darling, what would you like sung at the wedding?" asked Ben.

"I want, 'I Love you Truly' and 'Promise Me'. Do you have a special song, Ben?"

"I like 'The Lord's Prayer' and 'Hava La Gila' for the reception," said Ben. "I'm going to stop at the hotel to see if they have a suggestion for the band and the soloist.

"Ben, this has been a big rush, but I have had a lot of fun putting this together, and working with you."

"It's been exciting. We have really covered a lot of territory. I enjoyed working with you too. The best part of all, is that we'll be married and will be together for always," replied Ben.

"Darling! I love you!" declared Marta as she moved closer to Ben. He put his arm around her as they drove to Aunt Anna's. They went up to the door, to be met by Aunt Anna.

"I have a happy message for you," she said, "Dr. Thorson of the Lutheran Church said that he would be happy to marry you; however, he wants to meet with you tomorrow at 1 p.m. at the church. He wants to talk to you about the wedding ceremony."

Ben and Marta agreed to meet with him at that time. Then Aunt Anna had talked to the organist, who said that he would be delighted to play for them. He also would like to meet with you after Dr. Thorson talks with you at the same place. The church soloist is also available.

"Everything is falling into place. When this happens, I really believe that it's the Lord's will for us to marry," said Marta.

"I agree, "said Ben.

Ben and Marta had dinner with Aunt Anna, Uncle John and Inga. Ben left early, because he said that he had a lot of errands to run. He thanked them for the delicious dinner. He hugged and kissed Marta as he left.

Marta asked Aunt Anna if she was able to reach her sister in Upper Michigan. She said that she had reached her, but that they were unable to attend the wedding. Aunt Anna asked Marta if she had written to her parents. Marta said that she had planned to do that this evening.

Aunt Anna looked at Marta and said, "Why did you decide to marry so soon? Are you in trouble like Inga?"

"Oh no, Aunt Anna, Ben has never touched me in that way. The only reason that I was holding back before was because of the religion. Now Ben has agreed to have a Christian wedding, and he is open to our religion. He wants to study the New Testament with me. I'm praying that he will accept our Lord Jesus Christ as his personal Savior."

"I'm so glad," said Aunt Anna. "I like Ben, and respect him. I know that he'll make you a fine husband."

"Please excuse me now, as I want to write to my parents," said Marta as she got her stationary and began writing the letter.

> Dear Mother and Dad,
>
> By the time you receive this letter, I'll be married to Ben. I'm so sorry that you will not be present, but we can't wait any longer. We are so much in love.
>
> You will be happy to have Ben as your son-in-law. He is a very perceptive businessman. He and I are working together now. He lets me help in making the business decisions, and he likes my aggressive ways in the business world. He wants me to still be his business partner after we are married.
>
> Even though Ben is Jewish, he has agreed to have a Christian wedding.
>
> I love you and miss my brothers too. We'll be anxious to see you when you arrive. You are welcome to stay with Ben and I while you are looking for a place of your own.
>
> Love you,
> Marta

Then Marta went to sleep and dreamed of her life with Ben. It was a happy and secure life. She knew that she was doing the right thing.

When Ben arrived to pick her up, she told him that she would like him to drive her to the post office so that she could mail the letter. Then after that, they need to go to the jewelry shop to pick out a wedding band for him. They went to Tiffany's. Marta picked out the ring that she wanted for him. Then she had an inscription written on the inside of the ring. "To my love for always." Then they picked up their blood test results to take to the City Hall. They handed the results to the clerk and she, in turn, typed out the wedding license.

Then they went to the factory to see how the fittings were coming along. Everything was working out as planned. The dresses looked great.

At one o'clock, they walked into the church to find Dr. Thorson waiting for them in front of the church. He questioned them about their different faiths. Ben said that they had worked that out. "We're having a Christian wedding and a Jewish reception."

Then the minister asked them about the wedding vows. "Do you want the regular ways they are said?"

Marta said, "Everything is okay, but to change, 'to love, honor and cherish', instead of obey." She reminded the minister that they would have the dress rehearsal at 5 p.m. at the Waldorf Hotel, and dinner afterwards. She said that his wife was invited too.

Marta had a fitting for her dress at the factory, and did not want Ben to see the dress until the wedding. Ben promised not to go into the room where she was being fitted.

The dress rehearsal and dinner went just fine. The party broke up around 10 p.m. Marta and Ben kissed goodnight and she went home to pack for the next day. Ben's chauffeur would take care of the clothes she needed moved to Ben's after they were on their honeymoon. The Epsteins all had room at the Waldorf.

The day had arrived. Everyone was getting ready for the wedding. Marta was unusually calm. She looked stunning in her beautiful gown. Aunt Anna, Helen, and Inga fussed over her until everything was perfect. They drove to the hotel. Aunt Anna was ushered into the chapel. The chapel was tastefully decorated with pastel flowers and ferns. The wedding party carried white and colored orchids. The wedding march began, and Ruth was escorted by her husband to the front of the chapel. Then the bridesmaids came down the aisle. Mr. and Mrs. Epstein were already seated. Ben stood at the front of the church waiting for his beautiful bride.

He looked so handsome standing there looking so eager and attentive. In walked the ring bearer, followed by his sister who was dropping rose pedals down to the alter. The children were just darling - Josh in a miniature tuxedo and Sara in a beautiful floor length pink gown. Everyone stood when they saw Marta coming down the aisle. She looked so pure and innocent. Her gown was a creamy lace, fitted to her slender body; the back was quite full from the waist down. She had a train from her veil. Uncle John was so proud to be escorting his niece down to the man she loved. The minister asked, "Who gives this bride away?"

"I do," said Uncle John. Then he sat down, as the rest of the audience did the same.

When she got near Ben, he took her by the arm and led her to the alter where the minister was waiting. Ben whispered, "Marta, you take my breath away, you look so beautiful."

When they got to the kneeling rail, the soloist sang "The Lord's Prayer." Then the minister said a prayer about their union. As they said their vows, they looked into each other's eyes, and held hands. Then the soloist sang, "Because you come to me, with love...." Marta couldn't keep from crying. Tears were coming down her cheeks. Then the minister pronounced them man and wife. Ben lifted her veil and kissed her. The soloist then sang, "I Love You Truly." They then turned and faced the audience when the minister announced, "I now present Mr. and Mrs. Ben Epstein." They both had a big grin on their faces.

Chapter Fourteen

After the minister pronounced them man and wife, Ben lifted her veil and kissed her tenderly. Then they walked back down the aisle. The guests were given a small bag of birdseed to throw at them for good luck. After everyone shook hands with the bridal party, they sent the guests on to the reception while pictures were taken.

Hors d'oeuvres were being served with punch as the guests arrived. Mr. and Mrs. Epstein planned the reception. There was a band playing as the bridal party arrived. They played a waltz and Ben and Marta floated across the floor just beaming with happiness. Then Ben's father asked Marta to dance and Ben danced with his mother. Then the guests circled the couple and then a toast was made to the couple, Ben knew what to do with the glass. It was wrapped into a napkin, and when Ben smashed the glass with his heel, they shouted "Mozel tov" Then they played "Hava Nagila" and they all joined hands to dance to the music. Then Mr. Epstein asked everyone to take their places at the tables to eat a scrumptious luncheon. The best man gave a toast, "May you have a long happy life and be blessed with many lovely children." Everyone cheered as the bride and groom kissed. The guests were busy visiting and enjoying their food. Then the wedding cake was rolled into the room. Ben fed Marta a bite, and then Marta did likewise. Then the cake was served to the guests.

It was about 3 p.m. when Ben and Marta escaped from the crowd and took the elevator up to the bridal suite. Ben opened the door, and carried Marta over the threshold. He put her down and they both sat down on the couch. They sighed a breath of relief "At last," said Ben, "I have you all to myself. Can you believe it? We did it! Are you happy, Mrs. Epstein?"

"Ben, I am so happy. Can't you tell? I like being Mrs. Ben Epstein.

Just then, Ben got up and walked into the bedroom for a box for Marta. He handed her an oblong box. It was a beautiful necklace of emeralds and diamonds. "Oh, Ben! What an exquisite gift. In fact it is a perfect match to the bracelet that you gave me for Christmas." Then she hugged and kissed him.

"Just a minute, sweetheart, I have something for you too, "she said as she walked over to her suitcase.

Ben was surprised to see a square gold pocket watch. He opened it and said, "What a beautiful watch. I can wear it tomorrow with my vest." He always wore a vest with his suits, and he knew that it was both practical and very attractive. He held her and kissed her for a long time. "Hey, why don't we get into something more comfortable?"

"Ben, can you help me with all of these buttons?" asked Marta. By the time he finished, he began kissing her neck and her back. "Come on, Ben, you're not playing fair. Let me get into my gown and negligee."

"I hate to let you go, but if you must - you're mine now you know," he teased.

Marta held his face in her hands and kissed him all over. As she did, she whispered, "I love you, I love you," for each kiss. Then she broke away and went into the bedroom to change.

When she opened the door, Ben had removed his jacket, vest and was removing his tie. He met her halfway, carried her back into the bedroom, and put her on the bed. Marta slid between the sheets. Ben hurriedly removed his clothing. Marta closed her eyes, because she was afraid to look. Then he crawled into the bed too. He was breathing heavily. They met in the middle of the bed, and began kissing each other, as he did this he felt her breasts then lowered his head and traced his tongue around her nipples. This was all new to her, but she was enjoying the strange sensations that she was getting. She could feel his arousal on her leg, as he moved closer to remove her gown, and negligee. She wanted to feel him too. She began nibbling on his ears as she felt his strong body. He began kissing her again on the mouth. They teased each other with their tongues. Marta began to move her hips toward him. She felt very warm between her legs. He lowered his touch to the nub that was swollen with desire. "Darling, I want you so much, I can't wait much longer. It's going to hurt you when I first insert it, but afterwards, you will enjoy it as much as I will."

Marta reached for him and felt his hard shaft. It felt like it was throbbing. "Oh Ben, I want you too." Then she wrapped her legs around him as he inserted himself into her. At first, he was able to go just a little way, but then Marta gyrated and moved her hips wanting him to enter her. Then he pressed more when Marta felt a sharp pain. Ben stopped, but Marta urged him on. Finally, it was completely inserted. They were both enjoying the feel of the closeness. They moved together, and both came to unbelievable heights of passion as he poured his seed into her. They lay exhausted and wrapped into each other's arms when they both fell asleep. They awakened after a couple of hours later, and began to make love again. Each time it felt better, and they even reached more heights of love.

The next day, they awakened satiated in love. When Ben said that they would have to get ready to go the train station. They quickly bathed and readied themselves for their honeymoon. Ben had arranged for his chauffeur to carry their luggage and wedding apparel to the limo and drive them to the train station. They arrived at the station just in time. They were shown their compartment, just as the train started south for their honeymoon. Ben couldn't stay away from Marta even for a minute. They were on the seat kissing and hugging when the conductor knocked on their compartment door for their tickets. Ben handed him the tickets and asked if he would hang a sign outside of their door to not to be disturbed. "Honeymooner, eh? I'll be glad to oblige."

After a time, they decided to walk around the train to find out where everything was located, such as the dining car. They decided to have lunch in the diner. They could hardly wait to get back to their compartment so that they could curl up in each other's arm and make love again. The click clacking of the train rocking along the tracks soon lulled them to sleep.

They finally arrived in Palm Beach. It was warm and balmy. They had dressed in light clothes. Ben wore a white sport jacket, and Marta wore a white linen suit with a blue blouse. They were glowing. Two beautiful people in love. They made a striking couple. They were just glowing. He was tall, black hair and blue eyes. She came to his shoulders, auburn hair, and bright green eyes. Ben hailed a cab and they were taken to their Palm Beach resort. It was very impressive as they were driven to the door. The doorman opened the door for them and had the bellboy carry their luggage to the bridal suite. It was decorated in white furniture, trimmed in gold with a light blue carpet on the floor. Marta loved it as she walked all around to check on everything. They had a balcony overlooking the beach where they could sit and enjoy the view. After settling down and making love again, they decided to go down to the dining room. They ordered a large fruit salad and some iced tea.

The time went by fast. They relaxed, danced and made love.

Ben was so happy and so was Marta. In the evening, they dressed and went to the dining room that had a live band and dancing. Ben loved holding Marta in his arms and dancing.

After a couple days of pure bliss, they took a ship to the Bahamas. They did a lot of swimming and snorkeling. They stayed pretty much to themselves - they enjoyed each other's company found out more about each other.

Soon their honeymoon was over and they were heading north. "Ben, I really enjoyed Florida and the warm weather," said Marta.

"We can do this again, whenever you feel like getting out of the cold. Maybe later, we can buy a home down here for vacations. How would you like that?" asked Ben.

"I would love that. Then maybe our families could use the home too. It might be a nice place to have a family reunion. What do you think, Ben?"

"You are so thoughtful. Always thinking of your family, and making others happy. I love being married to you, darling," said Ben.

They stopped in Charleston, S.C. to order some new fabrics for their business. It was like being in a candy store. They were able to order all the fabric for the spring line.

They were able to catch their train on schedule. They settled into their compartment very rested, and looked forward to their trip home. As they were clacking down the tracks, they talked about redecorating Ben's home on Long Island. Ben told her that she would have to make the place more "Homey." They had received a lot of gifts and would have to unwrap them and send "Thank you" notes to everyone who sent them.

When they reached the train station in New York City, Ben's Chauffeur met them to drive them home. It was freezing and there was snow everywhere. The roads and streets were cleared, but it was very icy. Marta sat very close to Ben, and prayed that they would make it safely home. At last, they reached the front door. The butler and housekeeper met them at the door to welcome them home. The fire was crackling in the fireplace. It was so cozy, and they were exhausted from the trip. They bathed and soon fell asleep in each other's arms.

The next morning they received a call from Aunt Anna. She was very disturbed, because Uncle John had disappeared. He had been missing for three days. The police were notified, and there was no trace of him. She said that he was the last one to leave the store. The moneybox was missing too. He was going to get a cab to take him home. Ben told her that they would drive over to find out more of the details.

Marta and Ben were on their way within the hour. They could not imagine what could have happened to Uncle John. They found Aunt Anna worried and crying. She looked like she hadn't slept for days. Ben told her that he would hire a detective to look for him. Then he told her to pack up her things and come over to their home to live until things were better.

Inga had already moved to her husband's parent's house so that they could help her while she was expecting the baby. Aunt Anna was all alone so she was happy to pack up her things and move in with Marta and Ben. She sat down and wrote a note to John just in case he returned. She wrote to tell him that she was with Marta and Ben. She left the note on the kitchen table.

Sadly, she settled in with Marta and Ben. She waited patiently for word from her beloved husband. Ben had driven Helen and Anker's car to his home in Long Island.

Aunt Anna settled into Marta's guest room. She wasn't used to all of this luxury, but accepted it gratefully as she did not want to be in her home alone.

She told Ben about the detective Hank who lived near them, and that he had worked with Uncle John and Inga's husband during the time when they rescued the girls from the White Slavery ring. So Ben looked him up, and found out that he was missing too. The police were beginning to think that these two missing people were somehow connected to the gangsters' revenge.

After three weeks, there still was no sign of them. Finally, there was some news. The bodies had washed ashore. Anna was called to identify the bodies. This was difficult for her; of course, Ben and Marta went along for identification.

Everyone was concerned with the safety of the girls and the rest of the people who were involved. They were alerted to the situation, and were asked to be on guard.

Marta and Anna arranged for a funeral for Uncle John. It was a closed casket memorial service, because of the condition of his body. Helen and Anker were notified by telegram. They wired back to tell them how sorry they were, but were not able to attend the service. After the funeral, Aunt Anna gave up her townhouse and sold the store. Ben bought all of her sewing equipment and the sign above the store. He wanted to keep the sign as a memento for Marta.

After everything was settled, Aunt Anna decided to return to Upper Michigan to visit with her sister and to decide what to do next. Ben and Marta said goodbye at the train. They said that they would keep the car for Helen and Anker until they returned in June. It was sad for everyone. So much had happened to change everyone's life.

Marta heard from her parents. They were sad to have missed her wedding, but they were elated to hear that she was so happy and had her life dream fulfilled. They were anxious to meet Ben. They were selling the farm and would be in Upper Michigan by June. They suggested that Ben and Marta meet them there for a family reunion. Marta was delighted. She could hardly wait for Ben to return home so that she could tell him the news. When she heard him drive up, she ran to the door. He scooped her up in his arms and kissed her passionately. "I've missed you so much darling." Then she told him about the letter from her parents. He said that for sure they would go for sure. He said, "You can count on it."

Then they walked arm in arm to the library where Marta had tea and some biscuits ready for him. They talked about the business. Marta had been going to work about once a week. Now she wanted to participate more. It was March, and the cook planned on a mouth-watering dinner. They had the same menus that they had for their wedding reception. When they walked into the dining room, Marta said, "Happy third month anniversary!"

"I thought you may have forgotten, but I didn't." He said as he handed Marta a gift. They sat down and she opened the box.

"Ben, I love the way you spoil me." It was a beautiful diamond and emerald dinner ring. She sat on Ben's lap and handed him a box. Ben opened it, inside was a tiny sweater.

"Well, this is too small for me," said Ben, "It could only mean one thing. Are we going to become parents? When?" He hugged and kissed her on her neck.

"I'm two months pregnant. That means that our baby will be born in December," exclaimed Marta. "I haven't been sick at all! I think that babies agree with me."

"Have you seen a doctor?"

"Yes, I saw the doctor yesterday. I wanted to surprise you for our anniversary."

"I've been so busy with your uncle's disappearance and death that I haven't even thought about anything else. I'm so happy with the news. Now we'll have to plan for a nursery."

"I was talking to the detective that I hired to work on this problem with the gangsters who murdered your uncle, and Matt. This group is hard to trace. When someone is just about to be caught, they disappear. I'm leaving it up to the police now. I have dismissed the detective," said Ben.

"How are Inga and the girls getting along at the factory? Are they still afraid of the gangsters who kidnapped them when they first arrived in America?" asked Marta.

"Inga has been having some difficulty moving around. You know she is expecting her baby in June. She looks so lonely and sad. She really misses her husband. Why don't you invite her to visit for the weekend and let her talk about her problems? You two have something in common now."

"I'll have to talk with her when I go in tomorrow. Maybe she is also concerned about the gangsters. You know she blames herself for the deaths of the three men."

They were called into the dining room for a delicious dinner of roasted lamb. It was the exact dinner that was served at their wedding reception. They were so full that they decided to wait to have their dessert.

"Ben, I've been thinking of a new line of maternity clothes. Would you like to see some of my sketches? I just happen to have the sketches in the library. Come on and we can look them over."

"I do like them," said Ben. "You have designed some very comfortable dress clothes as well as everyday dresses. Bring in the designs and you can discuss them with the cutter and the other women who will be working on them."

When they went to sleep that night, Marta and Ben prayed for the girls who had been rescued from the gangsters and thanked God for their blessed event. They fell asleep in each other's arms full of love and anticipation.

The next day, they called Ben's parents to tell them of the great news. They were very excited. They were reminded again of their religious differences. Ben assured them that they would work it out.

That weekend Inga spent the time with Marta. She confided in the fact that she blamed herself for the deaths of the three men. "If only I hadn't escaped, and involved you with the gangsters."

"Don't blame yourself," said Marta, "Just think of the girls that you saved from the life of prostitution or even a horrible death." Then she held Inga in her arms as they both cried for their loved ones.

The weekend was healing for both girls. On Monday, all three drove into town to work. Marta was anxious to present her maternity designs and to get them ready for market. She was being selfish too, because she was beginning to need clothes for herself. They were busy discussing the clothes with the other workers when Ben peeked into the room and said, "I'm looking for my wife. Has anyone seen her?"

"Here I am," shouted Marta, as everyone moved away from the cutting table. Ben gave her a big hug, and said that he had missed her.

It was a beautiful spring day. Flowers were beginning to sprout. They were so happy together, enjoying everything that the new season had to offer. They decided to have lunch at a little restaurant near the park. In fact, they sat outside on the patio where there was a table and two chairs all set and ready for lunch. The crocus was peeking its head out. The daffodils were nodding their golden heads in the gentle breeze. The hyacinths were full of fragrance that only they could give. After lunch, they took a walk in the park. They walked along in silence, holding hands, enjoying spring and happy to be together.

The months passed by quickly, and her maternity fashions really took off. Why not? They had style and comfort. It was time to go to Upper Michigan for the Family Reunion. Marta was really feeling her pregnancy.

Inga had a beautiful baby boy. She named him Matthew, after his father. The boy had large blue eyes and strawberry blond hair. He weighed nine pounds at birth. His grandparents were very proud of him. He was a happy baby and it showed that he was loved. Inga decided to stay off work for three months. Then the baby could stay at home with his grandparents at the restaurant while she went back to work.

Helen and Anker arrived from Denmark. Ben and his chauffeur met them at the Ellis Island ferry. They drove to Marta and Ben's home. Marta met them and they both cried when they embraced. They were so sad about their father's death.

They were surprised to see Marta in a family way, but they were happy for them both. They decided to visit with them for a week before they started the long drive to Michigan.

Marta was beginning to really show. She was now four months along. She went to the doctor to see whether he thought it would be all right to take the trip. He told her that he felt that she would make the trip just fine. Anker and Helen asked her if they would like to travel with them in the car. Ben decided that it would be more comfortable for Marta to take the train. They could take a compartment so that she could lie down whenever she felt like it. So it was decided. Anker and Helen would drive and Ben and Marta would take the train.

The reunion was to be in two weeks. Marta and Ben decided to make arrangements to go a little early so that they could visit with her family. Ben had his father and mother move into their home to supervise the workers at the factory. They were glad for the opportunity, being retired they needed something for a change in their life.

Anker and Helen had a good rest at their home. They were treated royally. Marta got them tickets to see a Broadway show, and the Rocketts. They took them out for dinner before the shows. Of course, their cook provided them with delicious food daily. The following Monday they took off on their long drive to Michigan.

Marta and Ben were chauffeured to the train. They had a nice compartment. They were reminded of their honeymoon. The train took off on time chugging along to Chicago. From there, they would take a regular train to the Upper Peninsula. It would only take them one day from there, so it would not be necessary to have a compartment.

That evening they went to the dining room for dinner. As they were eating dinner, Ben noticed a sleazy looking man watching them. He hadn't thought of having protection. Ben and Marta talked about the reunion, and Ben did not want to alarm

Marta. When they finished dinner, Ben got up to escort Marta to the compartment. As they were leaving, Ben looked back to find the man getting up to follow them. Ben pulled Marta through the cars as fast as he could. He got to their compartment and locked the door. Marta said, "What's wrong Ben? You were rushing me so, that I almost fell."

"I'm sorry, Marta, I didn't want to alarm you, but I think that we are being followed by the Mafia, or one of the hoodlums of the Mafia. I hope that he didn't see which compartment that we went into. We will have to be very quiet. We'll go to sleep early so that I can get some help in the morning. Maybe I can wire the N.Y.P.D. and they can have someone meet us at the next city, or maybe in Chicago."

"Oh, Ben, I'm so frightened. I will pray and ask God for his protection. I'm worried about you and the baby."

"Don't worry, Darling. I'll protect you and the baby. Let's go to sleep now. We'll be in Chicago in the morning. Then I know that we will be safe. Ben stayed awake for most of the night. Marta was very tired so she fell asleep with the clacking of the train and the tracks. Early in the morning, Ben was dozing off to sleep when there was a loud thump on their door. They both woke up startled. Ben put his finger to his lips and signaled Marta not to speak. They were motionless. Then they could hear the conductor speak to someone in the hallway of the train. The conductor asked the man to move out of the area, because he would awaken the people who were sleeping in the compartments. They could hear the man move along with the conductor. Marta and Ben quickly got dressed and ready for the day. Ben was anxious to find the conductor so that he could wire ahead for protection in Chicago. He told Marta to keep the door locked and not to answer to anyone.

Ben walked out in search of the conductor. Only to find out that the entrance to the compartment had been watched by the gangster. The gangster followed him as he searched for the conductor. He saw him. Ben told the conductor that he was being harassed by the man following him. He told him that he needed to wire the police in Chicago so that he could have some protection. The conductor told him that he found the man pounding on Ben's compartment earlier in the morning. The conductor escorted Ben to the room where he could wire the N.Y.P.D. Then as he walked back to the compartment, he could not see the gangster. He was really worried about Marta, alone in the compartment. When he arrived, he found the door unlocked and the man holding Marta with a gun in her back. He said to Ben, "I will shoot your woman, if you give me any trouble. I want you to call off the cops in Chicago. If you do, I will let you go for now."

"I'm sorry, but that's impossible. The N.Y.P.D. has already been notified."

Just then, a security officer came to the compartment. "What's going on here? Drop the gun, or you'll be history." The gangster dropped the gun. He knew that he had a group meeting them at the Chicago station. The train security walked the man out. "I have a place all ready for you. You didn't know that we have a cell right here on the train. Mr. and Mrs. Epstein, I'm sorry that this scum has ruined your trip. We have a party waiting for him at the Chicago station. Enjoy the rest of your trip. He'll no longer be bothering you."

Ben and Marta thanked the security officer, and they ran into each other's arms. Marta began to cry, and Ben comforted her. "We have three more hours left until we arrive in Chicago. Let's go to the diner for breakfast."

"Okay," said Marta weakly. "It's not over, is it?"

"I'm afraid not," said Ben. "It's like a sore that won't go away. Let's forget about it now. Let's enjoy the rest of the day. I think that we will have protection when we arrive in Chicago."

They had a delicious breakfast, even though neither of them felt much like eating. Ben was worried about what was waiting for them in Chicago. If they are met by the police, they won't have to worry, but if they are not, that's something else again. He would have to keep Marta occupied so that she would not think of the danger.

"Darling, did you bring your sketch pad? I have been thinking of baby clothes. What do you think? Do you have any ideas?" asked Ben, hopefully. He knew that if Marta got busy sketching she would soon forget about the danger that they were in.

"Oh, yes," she said, "I've been already designing some. Would you like to see what I have been doing?" She whipped out her sketchbook. She had many designs of clothes from the Christening dress to rompers and play clothes. She kept busy with these until they needed to get ready for Chicago. They had their luggage ready for the porters. They sat in their compartment and watched as they came into the city of Chicago. The conductor came by, "Chicago! Out this way."

"I wonder if we'll see Tom working on the next train," thought Marta. "It would be nice to see a friendly face. I guess we wouldn't be seeing him anyway, because he would be working somewhere on the outside."

Chapter Fifteen

The police escorted Ben and Marta to the next train. They asked Ben if he would like someone to go with them to the Upper Peninsula. They said that they had the security officer who would keep an eye on them. Ben thought that this would be enough. He would contact the N.Y.P.D. when he arrived at Calumet, Michigan.

Ben and Marta enjoyed the countryside as they chugged along on the train. The countryside was beautiful with all the wild flowers in bloom. The hills were an emerald green. They reminded Ben of Marta's eyes. He was so concerned with the gangsters still out to get them for helping the girls that they had rescued from White Slavery. What would they do next? He would forget about them now. Perhaps the man that they caught would be willing to talk then they could get this thing resolved. He would find out as soon as he got Marta safely in the hands of her relatives.

It took all day, and Marta's ankles were beginning to swell. She tried putting her feet up on the seat ahead of them. Then she walked around for a bit, but still no relief. She was very uncomfortable. Ben took her feet into his lap and rubbed them for circulation. He said, "I think that we should find a doctor to have a look at your ankles tomorrow. I'm sure that Tom can refer a doctor to us."

"Oh, they'll be all right after I sleep tonight. It's been a long day. I have really enjoyed the countryside. We don't have much further to go." The conductor came by and told them that they would be arriving at their destination in half an hour. They sighed a breath of relief.

There they were, Marta's brothers! They hugged and kissed each other. Marta introduced Ben to them and they shook his hand. Then they got their luggage from the porter and carried them to the car. They brought two cars so that they would have room for everyone. Marta was so excited about seeing her family that she forgot all about her discomfort. They were taken to Aunt Sofi's home. They were going to stay with her family. They lived on a farm a little way out of the city. They had fields of strawberries just at the entrance of their driveway. Marta could see a little shed, and immediately knew that this was a sauna. There was a river close to the sauna where they could swim afterwards. She was anxious to introduce Ben to this Finnish treat. Everyone was there to greet them. Mom, Dad, and all the cousins, aunts and uncles were present. After the hugs and kisses and talking, her mother made Marta sit down while she had a look at her swollen ankles. She had some I.B.S. salve that she rubbed on her ankles. Then she wrapped her ankles. She made her put her feet up on the footstool and would not let her get up. They were served a delicious dinner. Uncle Al had the sauna ready. They let the guests, Ben and Marta go in first. Ben was a little afraid of Marta going, because of the long day. Her mother said that it would be good for her, because the swelling would go down.

Ben and Marta went out to the sauna. This was Ben's first experience. Marta told him about throwing water on the hot stones for steam. She also told him that she would sit on the bottom bench, but that he should go and sit on the higher bench. He said that he would prefer sitting with her. Marta saw a bunch of cedar on the bench. She picked it up and began switching herself. She started with her feet and legs. Ben watched her. Then he took a bunch also, and began switching himself. "This is for circulation," said Marta. They were all red and sweaty. "Now we'll take the tub of water and there was soap and wash cloths for them to wash themselves. After we wash, we'll go outside in the river and rinse off"

They helped each other scrub their backs. Then they washed their hair. "Are you ready to go outside to the river?" asked Marta.

"I'm ready!" said Ben, "Now I know how it feels to be roasted."

They made their way to the river. It was already dark outside, but they had placed a lantern so that they could find their way. The water was so refreshing. They walked into it and started to swim around. "This feels wonderful," said Ben. "I don't know when I've felt so relaxed." After about a half hour, they got out, wrapped a large towel around themselves and walked up to the house. They had a bedroom right near the entrance so they didn't have far to go. They got into their nightclothes and passed out. They slept so well that they didn't hear anything until the next day. They got up around 10 a.m., to the smell of bacon, eggs, and coffee. They also smelled the cinnamon rolls. They quickly got ready for the day. Ben was anxious to get in touch with the police, now that he felt that they were safe. Marta's legs were down to normal and she felt wonderful.

Aunt Anna was there and she was anxious to get an update on the gangsters who killed her husband. Ben told her of their experience on the train. He said that he was anxious to get in touch with the N.Y.P.D. to get an update on the gangster that was captured in Chicago. Uncle Al said that he would take him to the police station where they could call. Aunt Sofi did not have a phone.

Uncle Al and Ben drove to the police station. Ben explained the situation to the chief of police. He in turn, had the information from the police in Chicago. He told him that he was welcome to call the police in Chicago. They would update him on what was happening with the gangster that they picked up.

Ben called and talked to the chief of police in Chicago. He told Ben that the gangster was willing to talk if they would give him protection. They told him that if he would be a witness they would give him a new identification. He agreed to do this. "At last, we have a break!" said Ben.

The gangster said that the Mafia was out to get Ben and his wife, because of the involvement with the girls. "You need protection," said the police. "You're safe here, because as soon as we see someone strange in the area, and we have Marta's relatives who will be on the lookout too."

"I'll have to call the N.Y.P.D. to send someone to watch out for the girls who are working at my garment factory, and also my parents who are supervising the work," said Ben, "My home needs to have some protection too."

Ben and Uncle Al drove back to Aunt Sofi's house. They gave them the news. Ben was so worried about things back in New York. He told them that he would have to leave Marta with her family while he went back to New York to take care of things there. "I'll stay for a while," he said, "I'm worried about my parents and the girls at the factory. The gangster said that the other gangsters would not rest until we are all taken care of. Then they plan to take the girls back to prostitution. I feel that Marta would be safer here."

Marta went to Ben and said, "I'm sorry, Ben, but I want to be with you. I will worry about you if we are separated."

Her mother explained to her that he would be able to help the police to capture the men if he didn't have to worry about her. She finally agreed to let him go. He told her that he would be back as soon as he felt that it was safe for her to return home. He planned to leave in three days.

There was a knock on the door. It was Tom. He was very excited to see them both. He was surprised to see that Marta was pregnant. They had a good visit, and Aunt Sofi invited him to have lunch with them. He was so anxious to tell them about his job, and that he would be moving to Detroit soon. It was an advancement in his work. He was so sorry to hear about Uncle John's demise. Marta still felt butterflies when she saw Tom or even got near him, but she knew that she loved Ben.

The family reunion was to be the next day. They decided to have it in a nearby park. Everybody was to bring things that they cooked back in Finland. Marta was busy introducing her husband, Ben. All of the cousins, uncles, and aunts were there. They even sang Finnish songs. They played some of the Finnish music. Marta was so happy to be with her family. The food was very different to Ben, but he enjoyed everything. Aunt Sofi had picked the strawberries and had strawberry shortcake, which was enjoyed by all. Everyone was hurrying to clean up at the end of the day so that they could make it home before the mosquitoes came out.

When they reached home, Uncle Al had put smudge pots at the entrance of the house. They were pots filled with grass and lit with a match to produce smoke to keep the mosquitoes away. These, smudge pots were welcome. The mosquitoes were a real nuisance when they got near you.

The next day was when Ben would be leaving for New York. Marta clung to him in bed all night. Ben woke up to hear her sobbing. "Don't worry, Darling, I'll miss you terribly, but I want to take care of this big problem while you are safe with your family." He held her in his arms and kissed her tummy, "I love you, Marta. I don't want anything to happen to Baby or to you." They made love tenderly, and Marta soon fell asleep.

Uncle Al took Ben to the station. Marta decided to stay at home. She could barely say goodbye. Her eyes were red with tears. "Hurry back Sweetheart," she said.

Ben was heavy with sadness as he waved goodbye to his love. He had a premonition that maybe they would never see each other again. This uncertainty played on his emotions, and soon after he was on the train, he cried his heart out.

When Ben arrived at the New York Grand Central Station, he looked for his chauffeur. He was there all ready to take his luggage from the porter. They exchanged greetings, and Ben asked if his parents were doing well. He assured him that all was well on the home front. Then he inquired about Marta. Ben told him of the threat of the gangster on the train, and that he felt that it would be safer for Marta to stay with her family until all was settled here. The N.Y.P.D. was really busy trying to follow all the leads of the man that they captured in Chicago.

Just as Ben was stepping into the back of the limousine, a shot rang out and almost hit him. His chauffeur shoved him into the car and ran around to the driver's seat, entered, and locked all of the doors. Then sped off toward the police station. He could see a car following them, but when they pulled up at the station, they sped off in the opposite direction. They got out and walked right up to the Chief of Police. Ben told about the pot shot that was taken at him while they were at the railway station. The Chief of Police was very concerned. He told Ben that they had some good leads, and are working on them. They said that they would have an officer watch over him, and the factory. They would do the best that they can. Assured of their protection, Ben and the chauffeur drove to the factory. The girls were busy working. Ben's parents were there sitting in the office. They ran to greet him, and to find out why he hadn't brought Marta back with him.

Ben told them about the narrow escape that they had on the train. He said that even though they captured the gangster, he felt better leaving Marta up in Michigan with her family while he was trying to get to the bottom of the gangsters who were trying to get rid of them. He called the girls that were in danger to come into the office where they could talk in private. He told them of the events that led him back to New York. They were afraid to come to work. Ben told them that they would not hurt them, because they wanted to use them in the White Slavery Ring; however, they need to stay home until further notice. He told them never to go out alone, but always to go out in a group. They decided to close up the garment factory until it was safe for them. Then Ben took Inga and his parents home. Inga was taken to her in-law's restaurant. She wanted to be sure that her son was safe.

Ben's parents wanted to drive to their home. They felt that it would~ be safer for them to be far away from New York City. Ben had his chauffeur drive them home. It was lonely at his home on Long Island. He missed Marta, so he decided to send her a love note by telegram. He told her that he had arrived safely, but that he missed her very much. Then he told her that he was sending her 1 million kisses and hugs.

Marta was sitting at the table helping Aunt Sofi shell some peas for dinner. There was a knock at the door. She went to the door and to her surprise; there was a telegram from Ben. She was so glad to hear that he arrived safely and was happy to receive the kisses and hugs. She had a nice warm feeling. Also, she was having a lot of movement of her baby. It was such a thrill to feel the baby move. She felt so close to Ben. After all, the baby was a part of him. She went into the living room to tell her parents and her brothers that she had heard from Ben and all is well. She still had that gnawing feeling inside of her that told her that all was not well.

Marta tried to keep busy with her sketches, and helping with the household chores. A week went by, and she decided to take things into her own hands and return to her home on Long Island. She asked her brothers if they would accompany her. They were strong and could help in any situation. She asked Uncle Al to drive her to the telegraph station to let Ben know of her decision. When she went up to the window to give the message to be sent, they told her that she also had a message. They had given it to the Chief of Police. She sent her message and then rushed off the police station. The Chief of Police came to her and told her that he was on his way to her house.

He handed her the telegram. It informed her that her husband had been shot and is now in the hospital in very serious condition. She needed to come to him as soon as possible. She looked at Uncle Al and collapsed into his arms, in uncontrolled sobs. How can she get there fast enough? She wanted to be with Ben. They drove home and talked together. They called in Anker and Helen to discuss the fastest way that she could get to New York. They suggested that she take an airplane from Chicago. They said that they would drive her to Chicago and right to the airport. Now, Marta had never flown in an airplane, and she was frightened, but that was nothing to the desire to be with her loved one. So they planned to leave early in the evening and planned to drive all night. They would arrive in Chicago by noon the next day. Meanwhile, Anker, made reservations for her on the airline.

They wired a message to Ben's parents to meet Marta at the Airport by six in the evening. They received the message and Mr. Epstein met her at the airport. They rushed her to the hospital. Ben looked so pale, but when he heard Marta talking, he opened his eyes and reached out to her. "My Darling, I'm so glad you're here. I've missed you so much." Marta held him in her arms and showered him with kisses.

She saw the doctor arriving in the room. He motioned for her to come into the hallway where he could talk to her. "We were able to remove the bullet from his shoulder. He still has a lot of fever and weakness from the loss of blood. Now that you are here, I know that he will mend faster."

There were two police officers at the door so that he was well protected from the gangsters. They checked everything that was brought into the room. Even the flowers that were sent by his parents and from Marta's parents in Michigan.

Marta was very tired, but she would not leave Ben. Finally, Ben told her to get a room at the Waldorf so that she would be close to the hospital and would be able to rest. He asked his father to take care of this. Ben's parents were also staying at that hotel. She finally agreed to go for a couple of hours. Now that she felt that Ben was well attended and out of danger she thought of her baby, and the fact that she hadn't eaten anything all day. She went up to her room at the hotel and ordered a sandwich and a glass of milk. She took a quick bath, and found herself nodding. It didn't take long for her to fall asleep after crawling in between the sheets.

She slept until the early morning. She got ready to go to the hospital. She wanted to be there when Ben awakened, and find out when he would be able to go home where she could nurse him to health.

As she walked into the hospital, she noticed several police officers in the hospital. She went up to Ben's room. He was sitting up in bed having breakfast. "Darling, you must be feeling better."

"Yes, see what your being here has done for me," said Ben with his arms out to her. She walked up to him, gave him a hug, and kissed him all over his face.

Just then, the doctor walked in. "Our patient is doing much better. In fact, his temperature is normal. We may be able to send him home tomorrow."

"That will be wonderful," said Marta. She fussed around, fluffing his pillow, and clucking like a mother hen. She was where she wanted to be. Right next to her husband. He was shot in his left shoulder. His arm was in a sling. He was right-handed so he was able to feed himself

"Have you had breakfast?" asked Ben.

"Oh, no, I wanted to get here as soon as I could so that I could take care of you."

"I'll call the nurse and have her send you a breakfast. I'm sure that our baby is hungry too."

So Ben rang for the nurse and a half hour later, Marta was eating her breakfast too.

The day went fast. Soon it was time for Marta to go back to the hotel. She needed to send a telegram to her relatives in Michigan to tell them of Ben's recovery, and her safe trip.

The next day, at about 10 a.m. the chauffeur pulled up to the hospital to drive Ben, Marta and his parents to Long Island. The police escorted them to Long Island. The cook and butler welcomed them home. They were glad to see Marta too. Ben was able to walk around so that he could regain his strength.

He just wanted to have Marta with him all of the time. He loved her so much. At about noon, the butler came into the library and announced that the Chief of Police was there to talk to them. Ben told him to let him into the library.

The Chief of Police announced that their worries were over. They were able to find the gangster who was behind all of their problems. He confessed to having Uncle John, Matt and the private detective killed, and that he tried to kill Ben too. They all breathed a sigh of relief. Now they could get back to their life.

Marta was caught up on the designs at the garment factory. She said that she could take care of the shop while Ben was recovering. She needed to get her new baby designs out in the stores. Ben wanted her to stay at home with him, but he knew that she was determined to go back to work. "It will be okay with me," said Ben, "But I don't want you to run off just yet. I need your tender loving care."

Marta promised to stay home with him for another week. Then she just had to get back to work. After all, she would have to stop working when the baby comes. She made an appointment with the doctor to check on the baby's progress. The doctor informed her "Your babies are doing just fine!"

"What do you mean? Are you telling me that we are having more than one baby?"

"Yes, I hear two heartbeats," said the doctor. "You will soon have twins."

"No wonder I felt so big. It seems so difficult for me to walk around."

"It looks like you will have your babies in October instead of December," said the doctor.

"Oh, my that means that I am six months along."

She hurried off to tell Ben the great news. Ben was pleased to know that soon they would have two babies rather than one. His parents were still there and were just jubilant over the news.

While Ben was recuperating, Marta was working at the garment factory getting her new line of baby clothes on the market. Ben joined her after he stayed home for one month.

While they were having lunch in Ben's office, Marta had been having pains only about 10 minutes apart. In was October 15th. "Oh, Ben, I've been having pains 10 minutes apart. Now they seem to be coming faster. I think that you will have to call the doctor."

Ben took her to the couch to lie down. Then he called the doctor. He was told to rush her to the hospital. She was having twins, and she may have complications. So Ben quickly called the chauffeur, and informed the employees. They arrived at the hospital in record time - even before the doctor. She was put into a wheelchair and pushed up into the maternity ward. The pains were coming faster. The nurse prepped her and checked her out. They are coming fast. She told the other nurse to get the doctor immediately. Ben stayed by her side, until the doctor came and asked him to wait out in the waiting room. He walked over to Marta and kissed her. "I'll be praying for you," he whispered. "I love you darling."

Things happened fast after that. First one of the twins came, and the other right after that. The nurses took the babies and cleaned them up. Marta wanted to see them right away. "Are they all right?" she asked. "Do they have five fingers, and five toes?"

"They are beautiful! You have one red head, and one brunette! Both girls! Are you happy?"

"As long as they are healthy," replied Marta.

After everyone was cleaned up, and Marta was wheeled into her clean room, the babies were presented to her. Ben came in to see the beautiful sight. "How lucky can a guy be? I have three beautiful girls!"

They were beautiful. One looked so much like Marta and the other one favored Ben. They were a very happy family. The girls were raised with the knowledge of both religions. They were Christians, but they held on to many of the Jewish customs.